Emily Dickinson

献给孤独心灵的礼物

全彩珍藏版

这世界，静默如初

上

[美] 艾米莉·狄金森◎著

王晋华◎译

Selected Poems of

Emily Dickinson

台海出版社

灵性的自然

小女孩的秘园

难觅的知音

爱情的咏叹

欢愉与悲伤

静水流深

序言

Preface

艾米莉·狄金森（1830—1886年）和沃特·惠特曼（1819—1892年）一样，也是美国最伟大的诗人之一。他们两人生活在同一时代，都经历了美国的南北战争、波澜壮阔的民主运动和美国的文艺复兴，这些伟大的运动在气势恢宏的惠特曼的笔下都得到了生动的反映。惠特曼是时代的歌手，他全身心地投入到那一时代的洪流中去，并饱蘸着情感对其讴歌；而作为同一时代的诗人，艾米莉·狄金森的生活和诗歌则与惠特曼的完全不同。狄金森生长在一个富贵人家，一辈子没有结婚，很少交结朋友和参加社会活动，到了三十岁以后，更是足不出户，几乎隔绝了与外界的往来，与她的一个未嫁的姐姐终身相伴，过着孤寂无闻的生活。她几乎印证了我国老子“鸡犬之声相闻，老死不相往来”的名言。她的诗风也有与我国老庄相似的一面：淡名利轻生死，愿保持一种恬静澹泊的心境，愿过一种自然无为清心寡欲的生活，其诗也相应言简意赅，淳朴淡雅。她的诗歌在某种程度上说，是一种向内里反省的诗歌，是就平凡的日常事物进行哲理性思考的诗歌，在她的1775首诗里没有提到过当时社会上的重大的任何主题，没有提及现实生活中的任何重大事件，她的诗所探讨的毋宁说是一些永恒的主题：生与死，爱情，友情和亲情，名誉与财富，成功与受挫，理想与现实，灵魂与意识，希冀和追求，孤寂与天伦之乐，自由与束缚以及人生和经验等。她的诗不遵守传统的严密的格律，押韵也不像有些诗人那么严格，却十分讲究形象的具体性和含意，往往是透过一幕简短的情景便能暗示出人生的道理，为此她成为了20世纪英美意象派诗歌的先驱。下面我就艾米莉·狄金森诗歌里所表现出的一些主要观点做一简要的评述。

狄金森写了不少的诗歌来探讨人的心理。她认为人应该追求一种在灵魂和意识上的自由，人的心灵不应被生活中的任何痛苦和困境所压服，不应陷于日常生活的琐屑里而不能自拔，不要让追求物质享受的肉体羁绊了灵魂（参阅NO.384）。人最重要的是能超越自己，唯有超越了自己的人，才能战胜一切。正如作者在NO.1176中所说的：

我们从不知道自己有多么高大
直到我们应情势的需要而升起
……
我们诵颂不已的英雄主义
将会变为平常之事

只要不是因为我们怕当国王
硬是用腕尺羁缚了自己——

为此诗人要我们放飞我们的灵魂：

就像轻气球向大地只恳求
将它放飞而别无所望——
灵魂也愤愤然望着
尘封了它这么长时间的
泥土[①]

而且诗人认为人的高贵主要在其心灵：

外象——从内里
得到它的恢宏——
是公爵，是侏儒，取决于
其主要的禀性[②]——

高尚的人：

在他们离去时仿佛带走了什么

① 摘自其诗 NO.1630。
② 摘自其诗 NO.451。

就好像是——我们自己

蓦然间——失去了魂魄——

从这些诗句里我们可以看出诗人对心灵的自由和心灵的高尚是多么重视了。

其次诗人认为人应该有自信和信心（NO.766），有一个受内里驱动的那样一个目标作为自己不懈的追求（参阅NO.680，NO.750，NO.1099），要勇敢地探索，大胆地实验（NO.419），去不停顿地实现自己的理想（NO.1255），在这样做的过程中我们既要保持我们优良的传统，又要有创新的精神，像狄金森在其诗NO.839中所描绘的：

古老的优美品质，新颖的主题——

东方啊，你源自远古，

可是在你那紫金色的天幕上

每个黎明，都是新的一幕。

作为一个伟大的诗人，狄金森热情地歌颂真善美（NO.449，NO.836），不过她更强调自然之美，而摒弃雕饰之美，作者认为“美不能凭刻意求得”，美，“恰如草原上有风吹过时 / 草浪的翻滚起伏”，这是一种造化之美，淳朴之美。狄金森也颂扬那种真诚专一的爱情，那种你中有我、我中有你的爱情，那种精诚所至金石为开的爱情，其中 NO.453，NO.523 等笔者认为更佳，这些诗比喻新颖，格调清新，是狄金森的诗所独有的。

由于狄金森淡名利，所以她也能轻生死。因此当死亡这一主题从她的诗里表现出来时，就完全少了它平时给人的那种恐惧感，在她的诗里死亡倒能给人一种亲切和慰藉感。她的 NO.50，NO.182，NO.280，NO.294，NO.425，NO.1065，NO.1703 等诗都是探讨死亡的。读她的诗，像读老庄的文一样，可以减轻我们对死亡的恐惧心理。

在狄金森强调要过一种有理想有追求的生活，不要轻易放弃努力的同时，她并没有忽视了人生有无常，机遇有偶然性的一面（参阅 NO.1150，NO.1650），她在 NO.107 中写道：

这是一只很小——很小的船
在颠簸着驶出海港！
这是一个多浩瀚——多浩瀚的海
在招手邀它驶向远方！

这是多么贪婪，贪婪的海浪
在舔触着船儿离开海滨——
也不管有多少次航行
我的小船迷失在海中！

面对这一人生的无常，狄金森能保持一种逍遥和顺遂自然的乐天态度，像小石（NO.1510），小草（NO.333）那样，过一种恬淡闲适的生活。

上面我们就狄金森诗歌的内容做了一个大体的概括，当然其诗内容相当丰富，不是这短短的篇幅所能涵盖的。从形式说，她的诗歌的最大特点，就是善于运用具体的形象或比喻来阐释抽象的思想，揭示深刻的人生哲理，从她的诗歌里你能闻到“思想的玫瑰花香，”其诗 NO.764，NO.793，NO.875，NO.926，NO.928 等都是这一方面的代表作。这些格外清新、隽永的小诗，能给读者一种难以言表的美的享受。

王晋华

于中北大学外语系

2009 年 12 月 1 日

灵性的自然

Spirit of Nature

春鸟（NO.5）

我有只春鸟
它为我啭鸣啼叫——
并把春天引到。
每当夏季来临——
玖瑰花儿纷呈
这知更鸟儿就没了踪影。

不过，我并不懊恼
知道我的鸟
虽然飞走——
还会从大洋彼岸
为了我而归还
并带回新学下的曲调。

我的鸟儿所到的彼岸
人儿更善
风情更淳——
尽管它们现在离去，
我告诉我存怀疑的心府
它们不会把你摈弃。

I have a Bird in spring
Which for myself doth sing —
The spring decoys.
And as the summer nears —
And as the Rose appears,
Robin is gone.

Yet do I not repine
Knowing that Bird of mine
Though flown —
Learneth beyond the sea
Melody new for me
And will return.

Fast is a safer hand
Held in a truer
Land, Are mine —
And though they now depart,
Tell I my doubting heart
They're thine.

在一片更为安详的亮色里，
在一片更为辉煌的光照里
我看见
我心里的每一点儿
小小的恐惧和疑团
每一丝儿的忐忑和不安
都被驱散。

那时我将不会懊恼，
因为我知道我的鸟
虽然飞走
还会归来
栖息在这儿的树丛里
向我再展欢快的歌喉。

In a serener Bright,

In a more golden light

I see

Each little doubt and fear,

Each little discord here

Removed.

Then will I not repine,

Knowing that Bird of mine

Though flown

Shall in a distant tree

Bright melody for me

Return.

麻雀（NO.84）

她白嫩的乳胸前应戴上珍珠项链，
可我不是一个“潜水员”——
她的前额配得上王冠
可是我没有这样的冠冕
她的心灵温馨而甜蜜——
我——一只麻雀——用柔软的
枝藤在那儿搭起我
永久的窝。

Her breast is fit for pearls,

But I was not a "Diver" —

Her brow is fit for thrones

But I have not a crest.

Her heart is fit for home —

I — a Sparrow — build there

Sweet of twigs and twine

My perennial nest.

小小的玫瑰

没有人知道这朵小小的玫瑰——
它可能只是花儿沦落在郊野
如若不是我从蹊径边把它摘下
将它举到你的面前。
只有蜜蜂会对它思念——
只有蝴蝶，
从远途匆匆地飞来——
在它的花芯上落脚——
只有鸟儿会诧异——
只有风儿会叹嗟——
啊，小小的玫瑰——你的
花儿多么容易凋谢！

Nobody knows this little Rose —
It might a pilgrim be
Did I not take it from the ways
And lift it up to thee.
Only a Bee will miss it —
Only a Butterfly,
Hastening from far journey —
On its breast to lie —
Only a Bird will wonder —
Only a Breeze will sigh —
Ah Little Rose — how easy
For such as thee to die!

种子（NO.40）

当我心里数着播在
泥土里不久就会
将其花蕾绽放的种子——

当我细细地审视着那些
现在地位卑微
以后会受到尊重的人们时——

在我相信着世人们
不会看到的花园——
凭着信念摘取着它里面的花朵
并且避开了蜂儿时，
我便宁愿舍弃掉这美好的夏天。

When I count the seeds

That are sown beneath,

To bloom so, bye and bye —

When I con the people

Lain so low,

To be received as high —

When I believe the garden

Mortal shall not see —

Pick by faith its blossom

And avoid its Bee,

I can spare this summer, unreluctantly.

红装的花神（NO.74）

红装的花神——还像往年一样
在山里贞守着她的秘密！
素裹的花神，于田野中睡在
白色的百合里！

清爽的风儿用它们的笤帚
扫过河谷——山丘——和树林！
请告诉我，可爱的主妇们！[1]
你们在等待谁的来临？

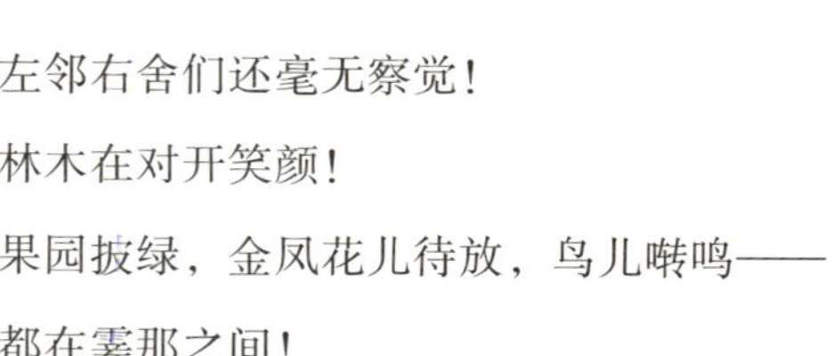

左邻右舍们还毫无察觉！
林木在对开笑颜！
果园拔绿，金凤花儿待放，鸟儿啭鸣——
都在霎那之间！

可是，秀丽的大地显得多么安静！
树篱又是多么的毫不在意！
好像这一“复苏”
是最平常不过的事！

---

① 比喻风。

A Lady red — amid the Hill
Her annual secret keeps!
A Lady white, within the Field
In placid Lily sleeps!

The tidy Breezes, with their Brooms —
Sweep vale — and hill — and tree!
Prithee, My pretty Housewives!
Who may expected be?

The Neighbors do not yet suspect!
The Woods exchange a smile!
Orchard, and Buttercup, and Bird —
In such a little while!

And yet, how still the Landscape stands!
How nonchalant the Hedge!
As if the "Resurrection"
Were nothing very strange!

它们隐伏在幽径里（NO.9）

它们隐伏在幽径里——荆棘草丛里——
隐伏在树林及林中的空地——
这些幽灵似的兽怪常常在
人迹罕至的道上与我们接踵擦肩。

野狼过来好奇地窥伺——
猫头鹰从树巅投下困惑的目光——
大莽的锦缎似的身躯
偷偷地溜过我们的身旁——

狂风掀起我们的衣襟——
闪电投下熠熠的光影——
从高高的巉岩上，饥饿的兀鹰
传下它凛厉的叫声——

树林之神在向我们招手——
山谷幽涧低低地嘟哝着“来，来呀”——
这些便是我们路上的伴儿——
就是在这样的路上
我们孩童飞似的跑回家。

Through lane it lay — through bramble —
Through clearing and through wood —
Banditti often passed us
Upon the lonely road.

The wolf came peering curious —
The owl looked puzzled down —
The serpent's satin figure
Glid stealthily along —

The tempests touched our garments —
The lightning's poinards gleamed —
Fierce from the Crag above us
The hungry Vulture screamed —

The satyr's fingers beckoned —
The valley murmured "Come" —
These were the mates —
This was the road
Those children fluttered home.

幽谷宝物（NO.91）

在我发现她[①]时她那么羞涩！
那么姣美——那么魂不守舍！
她藏匿在她繁茂的枝叶里
不愿让任何人发觉——

在我走过她时她连大气也不敢出——
当我踅回去要抱她离开
她又显得那么无助，
满脸绯红地不断地挣扎！

许多人定会问我为啥
要夺走这幽谷里的宝物——
我为啥要对这山谷背信弃义，
只是我永远不会说出！

---

① 代指一种少见的花。

So bashful when I spied her!
So pretty — so ashamed!
So hidden in her leaflets
Lest anybody find —

So breathless till I passed here —
So helpless when I turned
And bore her struggling, blushing,
Her simple haunts beyond!

For whom I robbed the Dingle —
For whom I betrayed the Dell —
Many, will doubtless ask me,
But I shall never tell!

雏菊（NO.106）

雏菊悄悄地追随着太阳——
当金色的太阳结束了他一天的徜徉——
雏菊便羞怯地坐在他的脚边——
太阳——醒来——发现了雏菊——
嗨——为什么——你在这里留宿？
先生，是甜蜜的爱情使然！

我们是花朵——你是太阳！
请你来把我们原谅——
如果我们在日暮时偷偷地挨你更近！
我们的魂儿迷恋着你要落下的西天——
因为平和——飘逸——美丽的紫色在那边展现
还有对与你相伴的夜晚的种种憧憬！

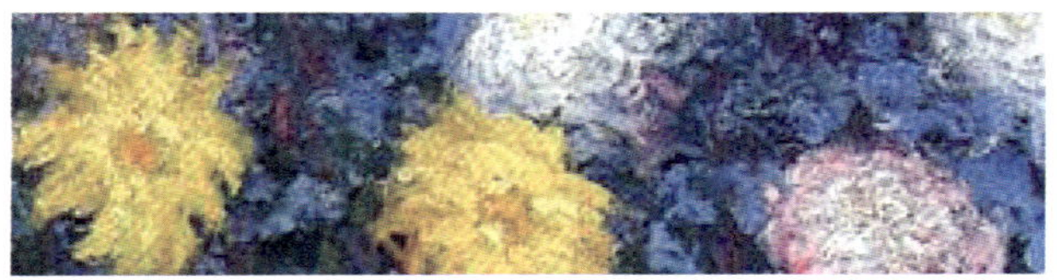

The Daisy follows soft the Sun —
And when his golden walk is done —
Sits shyly at his feet —
He — waking — finds the flower there —
Wherefore — Marauder — art thou here?
Because, Sir, love is sweet!

We are the Flower — Thou the Sun!
Forgive us, if as days decline —
We nearer steal to Thee!
Enamored of the parting West —
The peace — the flight — the Amethyst —
Night's possibility!

百合花（NO.392）

穿过黑暗的泥土（此为她所受的教育）——
百合花现在伸直了腰身——
她发觉她白色的枝茎——毫不颤栗——
她的信心——很是坚定——

后来，在草原上——在山谷里——
她欣然陶然地摇曳起
她海绿色的——钟状花冠——
全然忘记了在地底下的倒楣日子——

Through the Dark Sod — as Education —

The Lily passes sure —

Feels her white foot — no trepidation —

Her faith — no fear —

Afterward — in the Meadow —

Swinging her Beryl Bell —

The Mold-life — all forgotten — now —

In Ecstasy — and Dell —

花蕾（NO.133）

就像孩子们跟客人们道了“晚安”
舍不得离去一样——
我的花蕾也会噘起它们可爱的嘴唇——
因为又披上了它们的睡装。

就像孩子们醒来看到是早晨
欢喜得雀跃起来一样——
我的花蕾也会从花架上瞧下来
绽开它们妖艳的面庞。

As Children bid the Guest "Good Night"
And then reluctant turn —
My flowers raise their pretty lips —
Then put their nightgowns on.

As children caper when they wake
Merry that it is Morn —
My flowers from a hundred cribs
Will peep, and prance again.

一只受伤的鹿（NO.165）

一只受伤的鹿——会奔跳得老高——
我曾听猎人们这样对我讲——
这是死亡的幻觉使然——
很快它就又会平静得像往常！

被敲击的岩石会四处迸溅！
受踩踢的钢筋会弹了起来！
面颊总是赧红着
当激奋刺碰着心儿时！

欢悦是痛楚的铠甲——
痛苦小心地在里面武装。
免得让人们窥到鲜血
叫嚷起“你受到了创伤”！

A Wounded Deer — leaps highest —
I've heard the Hunter tell —
'Tis but the Ecstasy of death —
And then the Brake is still!

The Smitten Rock that gushes!
The trampled Steel that springs!
A Cheek is always redder
Just where the Hectic stings!

Mirth is the Mail of Anguish
In which it Cautious Arm,
Lest anybody spy the blood
And "you're hurt" exclaim!

草莓（NO.251）

草莓的枝儿
探过了——篱笆——
我能爬过——
树篱——如果我去试的话——
草莓的味道多么香甜！

可是倘若我弄脏了我的围裙——
上帝一定会把我责骂！
噢，天呀！——我猜想如果他是个男孩——
如果他能——他也会——去爬！

Over the fence —
Strawberries — grow —
Over the fence —
I could climb — if I tried, I know —
Berries are nice!

But — if I stained my Apron —
God would certainly scold!
Oh, dear, — I guess if He were a Boy —
He'd — climb — if He could!

小草没有什么事情可做（NO.333）

小草没有什么事情可做——
只是将一片绿色呈现
仅有蝴蝶飞来孵卵
蜜蜂前来嬉玩

小草整天和着风儿吹出的
曲调摇曳——
把阳光揽在它的怀抱里
向过路的人们弯腰致意——

晚上时，连起珍珠般的露水串串
把自己装扮得那么娇美
连公爵夫人也会显得寒伧
面对这样的景致——
即便在它衰朽以后——仍然发出

即便在它衰朽以后——仍然发出
圣洁的芳香——
犹如匍匐生长的香料植物进入睡乡，
又犹如甘松在消亡——

临了，它居住在高大宽敞的仓谷里——
小草真是逍遥，
做着梦儿打发着时光
我希望我也是一棵小草——

The Grass so little has to do —
A Sphere of simple Green —
With only Butterflies to brood
And Bees to entertain —

And stir all day to pretty Tunes
The Breezes fetch along —
And hold the Sunshine in its lap
And bow to everything —

And thread the Dews, all night, like Pearls —
And make itself so fine
A Duchess were too common
For such a noticing —

And even when it dies — to pass

In Odors so divine —
Like Lowly spices, lain to sleep —
Or Spikenards, perishing —

And then, in Sovereign Barns to dwell —
And dream the Days away,
The Grass so little has to do
I wish I were a Hay —

有多少花儿凋谢在林地（NO.404）

有多少花儿凋谢在林地——
或是消失在山野——
而从未有机会知道
它们自己的美丽——

有多少叫不出名儿的豆荚
乘着来风飞起——
而从未意识到在别人眼里它们红红的身体
飞过大地时有多么娇美——

How many Flowers fail in Wood —
Or perish from the Hill —
Without the privilege to know
That they are Beautiful —

How many cast a nameless Pod
Upon the nearest Breeze —
Unconscious of the Scarlet Freight —
It bear to Other Eyes —

黑色的浆果（NO.554）

黑色的浆果——虽然腹内有针刺——
可是没有人听到过他痛苦的呻吟——
他把他的果实，照样地
奉献给鹧鸪——和孩子们——

有时他将自己的身体倚着篱笆——
有时他挣扎着去攀附一棵树——
或者用他的两只手把岩石搂抱——
不过却不是为了把痛苦倾诉——

我们往往——说出伤痛——以求得慰藉——
而值得怜悯的他——只是
向天空——进一步地探起身子——
黑色的浆果勇敢又无畏——

The Black Berry — wears a Thorn in his side —
But no Man heard Him cry —
He offers His Berry, just the same
To Partridge — and to Boy —

He sometimes holds upon the Fence —
Or struggles to a Tree —
Or clasps a Rock, with both His Hands —
But not for Sympathy —

We — tell a Hurt — to cool it —
This Mourner — to the Sky
A little further reaches — instead —
Brave Black Berry —

自然（NO.668）

“自然”[①] 是我们眼见到的一切——
山峦——下午和傍晚——
松鼠——月蚀——营营的蜜蜂——
唔——自然是我们头顶的蓝天——
自然是我们的耳朵所听到的——
食米鸟的啼声——大海的涨息
雷鸣——蟋声——
唔——自然是和谐——
自然为我们所感所知——
可我们却说她不出——
我们的智慧是如此的苍白无力——
面对她的淳朴。

① 这是指造化而言。

"Nature" is what we see —

The Hill — the Afternoon —

Squirrel — Eclipse — the Bumble bee —

Nay — Nature is Heaven —

Nature is what we hear —

The Bobolink — the Sea —

Thunder — the Cricket —

Nay — Nature is Harmony —

Nature is what we know —

Yet have no art to say —

So impotent Our Wisdom is

To her Simplicity.

藏匿（NO.89）

树叶对着我敏感的耳朵——诉说——
灌木——犹如摇曳的铃铛——
四下都是大自然的哨兵
我找不到隐藏自己的地方——

如果我想要躲进山洞
洞壁——又打开了话匣子——
里面好像到处是大的裂缝——
使我无从藏匿——

To my quick ear the Leaves — conferred —
The Bushes — they were Bells —
I could not find a Privacy
From Nature's sentinels —

In Cave if I presumed to hide
The Walls — begun to tell —
Creation seemed a mighty Crack —
To make me visible —

它开放凋谢在一个中午（NO.395）

它开放凋谢在一个中午——
这朵鲜艳的红红的花——
经过的我想，再一个中午
另一朵花便会替代了它

并发出同样的光彩，随后就忘掉了它
另一天我又走过这里，
却发现这一花种全然消失了——
尽管在此地——

太阳仍一样的绚丽——花木
一样的争艳——
倘若我那天能驻足逗留
现在的我感到了无尽的遗憾——

有多少这一地带和其他地方的花卉
在我手中枯萎
为了寻找这许多花与它之间的相似——
可我却无法找到它的匹配——

地球上的这枝独特的花
我在经过它时，还不明白：
大自然的面容——千姿百态
在我面前永不重复地展开——

It bloomed and dropt, a Single Noon —
The Flower — distinct and Red —
I, passing, thought another Noon
Another in its stead

Will equal glow, and thought no More
But came another Day
To find the Species disappeared —
The Same Locality —

The Sun in place — no other fraud
On Nature's perfect Sum —
Had I but lingered Yeste rday —
Was my retrieveless blame —

Much Flowers of this and further Zones
Have perished in my Hands
For seeking its Resemblance —
But unapproached it stands —

The single Flower of the Earth
That I, in passing by
Unconscious was — Great Nature's Face
Passed infinite by Me —

蛇（NO.986）

一条细细的家伙[①]有时
会在草里穿行——
你也许碰到过他——不是吗
他的出现突然得很——

草丛像是梳过得一般向两边分开
现出草叶斑驳的通道一条——
当草丛在你脚下合拢了时
它又在前面分出了道——

他喜欢沼泽似的地域
这阴湿地可不适于玉米的种植——
在童年时，于中午时分——
我光着脚不只一次

① 指蛇。

A narrow Fellow in the Grass

Occasionally rides —

You may have met Him — did you not

His notice sudden is —

The Grass divides as with a Comb —

A spotted shaft is seen —

And then it closes at your feet

And opens further on —

He likes a Boggy Acre

A Floor too cool for Corn —

Yet when a Boy, and Barefoot —

I more than once at Noon

走过这儿，以为看到一根
缠开了的鞭梢在阳光里
当我俯身要捡起时
它却身子一缩，不知溜到了何地——

我认识好几个自然之子
他们对我也很熟悉——
他们的纯真率直总会令我
心旷神怡——

可是每当我遇到他[①]时
不管我是有人相随还是单独一人
我都会屏住呼吸
从骨子里面发冷——

① 指蛇。

Have passed, I thought, a Whip lash
Unbraiding in the Sun
When stooping to secure it
It wrinkled, and was gone —

Several of Nature's People
I know, and they know me —
I feel for them a transport
Of cordiality —

But never met this Fellow
Attended, or alone
Without a tighter breathing
And Zero at the Bone —

叶子的秘语（NO.987）

树上的叶子像女人们那样互相
倾诉着心腹话儿——
有时是相互点头，有时是
神秘的悄语。

无论是树叶还是女人们
都乐于享有他们之间的秘密——
永不会违约
向外宣示。

The Leaves like Women interchange
Exclusive Confidence —
Somewhat of nods and somewhat
Portentous inference.

The Parties in both cases
Enjoining secrecy —
Inviolable compact
To notoriety.

眼前的快乐（NO.1080）

当花儿再度争艳的时候——假如它们会——
我总有这样的一个怀疑
花卉是否还能再生
如果艺术一旦逝去——

当知更鸟开始啼唱的时候，假如它们会——
我总有一个担心
我不知道这会不会是它们
最后的一次啼鸣，

当五月又来临的时候，假如它会——
难道不会有人暗自心伤：
这会不会是他最后一次看到
大自然如此美丽的面庞？

如果我在那儿[①]——一个人不知道
他明天的命运将会如何——
不过如果我在那儿，我会丢掉前面的
种种担心去尽享眼前的快乐——

① 指再度身临上面的种种美妙处。

When they come back — if Blossoms do —
I always feel a doubt
If Blossoms can be born again
When once the Art is out —

When they begin, if Robins may,
I always had a fear
I did not tell, it was their last Experiment
Last Year,

When it is May, if May return,
Had nobody a pang
Lest in a Face so beautiful
He might not look again?

If I am there — One does not know
What Party — One may be
Tomorrow, but if I am there
I take back all I say —

化蝶（NO.1099）

我的茧衣变紧——颜色也变得好怪——
我摸索着想吸到空气——
一种于朦胧中长翮羽的力
弄坏了裹在我身上的靓衣——

蝴蝶的力量须体现在
它擅于飞翔
须隐含了在浩瀚无垠的草原
和天空能任意地徜徉——

起初我对这一暗示感到困惑
拼力去破释其间的奥秘
趺趺撞撞摔了不少的跤，直到最后
我领悟了那一神圣的提示——

My Cocoon tightens — Colors tease —
I'm feeling for the Air —
A dim capacity for Wings
Demeans the Dress I wear —

A power of Butterfly must be —
The Aptitude to fly
Meadows of Majesty implies
And easy Sweeps of Sky —

So I must baffle at the Hint
And cipher at the Sign
And make much blunder, if at least
I take the clue divine —

三叶草（NO.1232）

三叶草的小小名声
虽然只有乳牛记得
却也胜过经过包装添彩的
声名远播。

如若名声察觉到了它自己
那会有损于花的芬芳
回头频频顾盼的雏菊
已经减弱了它的力量

The Clover's simple Fame
Remembered of the Cow —
Is better than enameled Realms
Of notability.

Renown perceives itself
And that degrades the Flower —
The Daisy that has looked behind
Has compromised its power —

蜜蜂与玫瑰花（NO.1339）

蜜蜂驭着他锃亮的车驾
大胆地奔向了玫瑰花——
并将他和他的车子——一起
在她的上面落了脚——

玫瑰坦诚温静地
将他的造访接受
不对贪婪的蜜蜂
把一个花瓣保留

他们之间的销魂的时刻很快结束——
随即蜜蜂——逃得没了影子——
剩下的花儿——还在陶然欣然地回味
不过却多了一份谦卑。

A Bee his burnished Carriage
Drove boldly to a Rose —
Combinedly alighting —
Himself — his Carriage was —

The Rose received his visit
With frank tranquillity
Withholding not a Crescent
To his Cupidity —

Their Moment consummated —
Remained for him — to flee —
Remained for her — of rapture
But the humility.

坚果的衣服（NO.1371）

坚果的裁缝如何会把他的深色外衣
裁制得这么合适？
连接得没有一条缝隙
就像梦中之靓衣——

是谁纺成了这赭色的布？
合身的腰围又是如何算出？
因为这身古朴的衣衫
栗子一直要穿到老年

我们知道我们有智慧——
做出的成就令人惊奇——
可是与造化和这位乡下佬[①]——
相比——我们又是多么渺小！

① 指坚果的裁缝。

How fits his Umber Coat
The Tailor of the Nut?
Combined without a seam
Like Raiment of a Dream —

Who spun the Auburn Cloth?
Computed how the girth?
The Chestnut aged grows
In those primeval Clothes —

We know that we are wise —
Accomplished in Surprise —
Yet by this Countryman —
This nature — how undone!

飘雪（NO.1075）

天幕低垂——云层黯淡
一片飘舞的雪花儿
正拿不定主意，不知它是该
飘过谷仓还是穿过车辙——

一股小心眼儿的风一整天地抱怨
有人如何地不把他善待
大自然像我们一样有时也会让人瞥见
她不戴王冠的样态。

The Sky is low — the Clouds are mean.
A Travelling Flake of Snow
Across a Barn or through a Rut
Debates if it will go —

A Narrow Wind complains all Day
How some one treated him
Nature, like Us is sometimes caught
Without her Diadem.

冰封（NO.519）

起初——它也像我们——充满温暖
直到料峭的寒意
悄然来至——宛如冰霜结在了镜面——
一切都在萧杀中——逝去。

前额僵硬如石——
手指变凉失去痛觉
宛若——封冻的溪流——
灵动的眼睛——变得呆滞——

它失去了柔韧——仅此而已
它把淡漠变本加厉——
把寒冷蓄积得无以复加——
因为高傲已是它的一切——

哪怕用绳子平衡——
它仍旧下沉，恍若一份负重——
它没有发出信号，也没有提出异议，
而是像顽石一样地坠落。

Twas warm — at first — like Us —
Until there crept upon
A Chill — like frost upon a Glass —
Till all the scene — be gone.

The Forehead copied Stone —
The Fingers grew too cold
To ache — and like a Skater's Brook —
The busy eyes — congealed —

It straightened — that was all —
It crowded Cold to Cold —
It multiplied indifference —
As Pride were all it could —

And even when with Cords —
'Twas lowered, like a Weight —
It made no Signal, nor demurred,
But dropped like Adamant.

露珠（NO.1437）

一颗适意自得的露珠——
欣怡了一片绿叶
同时也感到了“命运的无常”——
“生命的卑微！”

太阳升起在天空照耀——
白昼也出来嬉玩
不一会儿那颗露珠的形体
我们便不再看得见

是白天掠走了它
还是太阳
将它送到了大海，对此
我们将永远无从知晓

这个可悲的事实
在对我们宣示
命运的多变
和厄运到来的迅疾。

A Dew sufficed itself —
And satisfied a Leaf
And felt "how vast a destiny" —
"How trivial is Life!"

The Sun went out to work —
The Day went out to play
And not again that Dew be seen
By Physiognomy

Whether by Day Abducted
Or emptied by the Sun
Into the Sea in passing
Eternally unknown

Attested to this Day
That awful Tragedy
By Transport's instability
And Doom's celerity.

太阳（NO.1190）

太阳和大雾在争夺着
对白昼的支配权——
太阳甩起他那金黄色的鞭梢
把雾霭驱散——

The Sun and Fog contested
The Government of Day —
The Sun took down his Yellow Whip
And drove the Fog away —

落日（NO.764）

预感——是草地上的——长长的投影——
指示出太阳正在西沉

告诉受到惊扰的青草
黑夜——即将来到——

Presentiment — is that long Shadow — on the Lawn —
Indicatives that Suns go down —

The Notice to the startled Grass
That Darkness — is about to pass —

曲调（NO.1389）

轻轻地拨动大自然的美好琴弦
如果你不懂得它的曲调
否则每一只鸟儿都会指着你
嫌你这位诗人太毛躁——

Touch lightly Nature's sweet Guitar
Unless thou know'st the Tune
Or every Bird will point at thee
Because a Bard too soon —

不要太走近玫瑰的花蕾（NO.1434）

不要太走近玫瑰的花蕾——
一阵风儿的吹拂
几多露水的浸润
便能惊得它们落红无数——

不要企图去系住蝴蝶
不要爬上狂喜的栏杆
尚未在掌握之中
是快乐得以确保的源泉。

Go not too near a House of Rose —
The depredation of a Breeze —
Or inundation of a Dew
Alarms its walls away —

Nor try to tie the Butterfly,
Nor climb the Bars of Ecstasy,
In insecurity to lie
Is Joy's insuring quality.

你好，子夜（NO.425）

你好——子夜——
我回来啦——
白昼——已经厌倦了我——
我怎么会讨厌了他呢？

阳光明媚的地方当然好——
我愿意在那里流连——
可是早晨——现在——不再想要我了——
所以——再见吧——白天！

我喜欢眺望——不是吗？——
在东方泛红的时刻——
那时——群山——呈现出一派气象——
能使心灵——开阔——

你——没有那般美好——子夜——
我愿意拥有——白日——
不过——请你留下一个小女孩——
既然他已把我摈弃！

Good Morning — Midnight —

I'm coming Home —

Day — got tired of Me —

How could I — of Him?

Sunshine was a sweet place —

I liked to stay —

But Morn — didn't want me — now —

So — Goodnight — Day!

I can look — can't I —

When the East is Red?

The Hills — have a way — then —

That puts the Heart — abroad —

You — are not so fair — Midnight —

I chose — Day —

But — please take a little Girl —

He turned away!

美（NO.516）

美——不能刻意——求得——
你追它，它便没了踪影——
你不追，它倒留住了脚儿——
并为你拂去凿痕

恰如草原上——有风吹过时
草浪的翻滚起伏——
这一自然之造化
我们怎能僭越——

Beauty — be not caused — It Is —

Chase it, and it ceases —

Chase it not, and it abides —

Overtake the Creases

In the Meadow — when the Wind

Runs his fingers thro' it —

Deity will see to it

That You never do it —

我的花束是送给囚禁者（NO.95）

我的花束是送给囚禁者——
他们的眼睛总是充满朦胧的期待，
他们的手不能用来自由地采撷，
他们在怀着理想忍耐。

如果这些花束为他们
带去了清晨和旷野的讯息，
它们便完成了它们的使命，
我也不再有别的希冀。

My nosegays are for Captives —
Dim — expectant eyes,
Fingers denied the plucking,
Patient till Paradise.

To such, if they should whisper
Of morning and the moor,
They bear no other errand,
And I, no other prayer.

花园（NO.99）

新的足音踏响在我的花园里——
新的手指翻弄着这泥土——
榆树上有一只啼鸟[①]
把这儿的寂寥披露。

不认识的孩子们在草地上玩耍——
陌生的面孔睡在树阴下——
可令人惆怅的夏天照样来到
冬天莅临时雪花照样地飘洒！

① troubadour 是抒情诗人的意思，这里喻指啼鸟。

New feet within my garden go —

New fingers stir the sod —

A Troubadour upon the Elm

Betrays the solitude.

New children play upon the green —

New Weary sleep below —

And still the pensive Spring returns —

And still the punctual snow!

宝石（NO.245）

我把一块宝石攥在手心里——
然后渐渐地睡着——
那一天天气温暖，风儿和煦，
我念叨着“要把它保存好”——

我醒了——开始怪罪我忠实的手指，
宝石不见了
现在，一种对紫晶色的光儿的回忆
便是我所拥有的一切——

I held a Jewel in my fingers —

And went to sleep —

The day was warm, and winds were prosy —

I said "'Twill keep" —

I woke — and chid my honest fingers,

The Gem was gone —

And now, an Amethyst remembrance

Is all I own —

你心中有条潺潺的溪流吗（NO.136）

你心中有条潺潺的溪流吗，
那里有卑微的花儿摇曳，
羞怯的鸟儿飞下来呷水，
还有影子在微微的颤栗——

水流得那么静，谁也不知道，
会有条小溪在那里，
然而就是从这条溪里你每天
吮吸着生命的甘滴——

哦，你一定见过三月涨水的小溪，
那时河水溢出堤坝，
融雪从山上急泻而下，
常常把桥梁冲垮——

后来，到了八月的时节——
当草原敞起它焦裂的胸脯，
此时，你可要当心，以免生命的小溪，
干涸在一个炙热的中午！

Have you got a Brook in your little heart,
Where bashful flowers blow,
And blushing birds go down to drink,
And shadows tremble so —

And nobody knows, so still it flows,
That any brook is there,
And yet your little draught of life
Is daily drunken there —

Why, look out for the little brook in March,
When the rivers overflow,
And the snows come hurrying from the fills,
And the bridges often go —

And later, in August it may be —
When the meadows parching lie,
Beware, lest this little brook of life,
Some burning noon go dry!

雏菊花丛（NO.1037）

在这雏菊的花丛里是我的身体
最愿意躺下的地方
外面的每一棵摇曳的小草
都为我带上了少许的悲伤。

我将悄悄地告诉我的雏菊
哪里是我可能要去的地方——
哪些是我的朋友，他们
将会温存地待她[①]。

距离也不能把我
和她自己分开——
因为我们俩盛开在一朵花里
无论是我在，还是离开——

① 指雏菊。

Here, where the Daisies fit my Head
'Tis easiest to lie
And every Grass that plays outside
Is sorry, some, for me.

Where I am not afraid to go
I may confide my Flower —
Who was not Enemy of Me
Will gentle be, to Her.

Nor separate, Herself and Me
By Distances become —
A single Bloom we constitute
Departed, or at Home —

窗前（NO.327）

在我未合上眼睛的时候
我也和其他有眼的生物
一样喜欢观览，
这也是本能使然——

可是如果今天有人——告诉我——
我自己可以拥有整个
天空——我敢说由于我的渺小
我的心儿定会爆裂——

一望无际的草原是——我的——
叠嶂的山峰是——我的——
所有的森林——永远闪烁的星星——
还有在我有限的视野之内
所看到的一切——

呷水的小鸟的一俯一仰——
早晨琥珀色的霞霜——
都任我随意地眺望——
这样的好消息一定会把我惊呆——

所以——还是——把心儿只探在
窗台上猜想的好——
任凭其他的人在窗前
举目去远眺——

Before I got my eye put out
I liked as well to see —
As other Creatures, that have Eyes
And know no other way —

But were it told to me — Today —
That I might have the sky
For mine — I tell you that my Heart
Would split, for size of me —

The Meadows — mine —
The Mountains — mine —
All Forests — Stintless Stars —
As much of Noon as I could take

Between my finite eyes —
The Motions of the Dipping Birds —
The Morning's Amber Road —
For mine — to look at when I liked —

The News would strike me dead —
So safer — guess — with just my soul
Upon the Window pane —
Where other Creatures put their eyes —
Incautious — of the Sun —

惊（NO.323）

就好像我只求少许的施舍，
在我那颤巍巍的手中
一个陌生人硬塞给我一个王国，
我立在那儿，茫然无所从——
就好像我请求东方
能带给我一个早晨——
东方竟会掀起它那紫色的闸门，
把我浸没在晓光中！

As if I asked a common Alms,

And in my wondering hand

A Stranger pressed a Kingdom,

And I, bewildered, stand —

As if I asked the Orient

Had it for me a Morn —

And it should lift its purple Dikes,

And shatter me with Dawn!

小溪（NO.1200）

因为我的小溪在汩汩而流
我知道它已快要见底——
因为我的小溪缄默不语
我知道它已深似海水——

对小溪的涨起我很吃惊
我试着逃跑
逃到坚强的人告诉我
这儿已“不再有水潮”①

① 此诗喻作者想保持一种清明恬淡之心境。

Because my Brook is fluent

I know 'tis dry —

Because my Brook is silent

It is the Sea —

And startled at its rising

I try to flee

To where the Strong assure me

Is "no more Sea" —

小小的石头多幸福（NO.1510）

小小的石头多幸福
路上自个儿独举步，
功名利禄不在乎
也从不担心有祸福——
它那质朴的棕色衣
连瞬息万变的世界也得披，
它的独立不羁，像是太阳
随意地照射着它的光，
它全然顺应天意
单纯又无为——

How happy is the little Stone
That rambles in the Road alone,
And doesn't care about Careers
And Exigencies never fears —
Whose Coat of elemental Brown
A passing Universe put on,
And independent as the Sun
Associates or glows alone,
Fulfilling absolute Decree
In casual simplicity —

记忆（NO.1578）

鲜花会枯萎飘落，
珍馐美味只有一日的炫赫，
但是记忆像音乐
永远鲜活。

Blossoms will run away,
Cakes reign but a Day,
But Memory like Melody
Is pink Eternally.

好奇心

紫色的山峦在翘首聆听
河流在倚着身子眺望
可是人却没有好奇心
不像万物那样。

The Hills erect their Purple Heads
The Rivers lean to see
Yet Man has not of all the Throng
A Curiosity.

影子（NO.1105）

影子今天来到了小山上宛如
男人和女人们的样子
这里一个深深的鞠躬
那里一个长长的行礼
当然是对它们自己的邻居
然后步子加快——不予理会
像我们自己这样的小小景观
以及我们的居住之地——

Like Men and Women Shadows walk
Upon the Hills Today —
With here and there a mighty Bow
Or trailing Courtesy
To Neighbors doubtless of their own
Not quickened to perceive
Minuter landscape as Ourselves
And Boroughs where we live —

月亮（NO.1315）

哪一个最好——是圆月还是月牙？
都不是——月亮说——
最好的是还没有的——一旦实现了它——
你就除去了它的光泽。

“实现”不具有羁缚的性质
所以去获得时不会颤栗
只是其迷人的力量随即消失——
他[①]生来就是一个棱镜体。

Which is the best — the Moon or the Crescent?
Neither — said the Moon —
That is best which is not — Achieve it —
You efface the Sheen.

Not of detention is Fruition —
Shudder to attain.
Transport's decomposition follows —
He is Prism born.

---

① 指现实和成就。

春水（NO.1425）

春水的恣肆涨溢
开豁了每一个心灵——
它冲走了房屋
使水与天毗邻——

开始时心灵感到些许的疏隔——
依稀在寻找它的堤堰
不过一旦习惯——便不再想望
到达那个岛屿了——

The inundation of the Spring
Enlarges every soul —
It sweeps the tenement away
But leaves the Water whole —

In which the soul at first estranged —
Seeks faintly for its shore
But acclimated — pines no more
For that Peninsula —

宅第（NO.127）

“宅第”——聪明的人们这样对我说——
“宅第”！务必要建得舒适温馨！
巨宅不能叫泪水儿浸，
巨宅里不能让凄风苦雨涌进！

“这许多的巨宅”，是由“他父亲”建造，
我从没听说过他的名字！
孩子们能找到去那儿的路吗——
有的甚至在今晚的路途中就会迷失！

"Houses" — so the Wise Men tell me —
"Mansions"! Mansions must be warm!
Mansions cannot let the tears in,
Mansions must exclude the storm!

"Many Mansions," by "his Father,"
I don't know him; snugly built!
Could the Children find the way there —
Some, would even trudge tonight!

信心（NO.766）

我的信心比山还大——
所以在山塌陷之后——
我的信心必会驭着太阳的车驾
给太阳引路——

纵使太阳金色的脚步会走歪——
纵使鸟儿不再于早晨啼叫——
鲜花不再在枝条上摇曳——
天堂里不再有铃铛儿敲——

我也不敢因此把信心遏止
因为无尽的一切都依凭于它——
不能由于我这个立天柱上的铆钉松了——
而叫苍天坍塌

My Faith is larger than the Hills —
So when the Hills decay —
My Faith must take the Purple Wheel
To show the Sun the way —

'Tis first He steps upon the Vane —
And then — upon the Hill —
And then abroad the World He go
To do His Golden Will —

And if His Yellow feet should miss —
The Bird would not arise —
The Flowers would slumber on their Stems —
No Bells have Paradise —

How dare I, therefore, stint a faith
On which so vast depends —
Lest Firmament should fail for me —
The Rivet in the Bands

我丢失了一个世界（NO.181）

我丢失了一个世界——在那一天！
有人看到了吗？
你会认出它来，因为在它的前额上
有一排星辰环绕。

一个富有的人——也许对它不会注意——
可是——对于我寡欲的眼睛，
它比钱币更加珍贵——
噢，请帮我——找到它——先生！

I lost a World — the other day!
Has Anybody found?
You'll know it by the Row of Stars
Around its forehead bound.

A Rich man — might not notice it —
Yet — to my frugal Eye,
Of more Esteem than Ducats —
Oh find it — Sir — for me!

萌芽（NO.701）

今天有一个思想涌入我的脑海——
它以前也曾在我脑中出现——
只是还未成形——在萌芽状态——
我不能肯定那是在哪一年——

我也不知它后来去了哪里，不知为什么
它又第二次在我脑中闪烁——
我也没有本领确切地说出——
它是什么——

不过我知道在我心底的——什么地方——
我曾与它照面——
这次只是使我又想起了它——仅此而已——
以后它便再也没有出现——

A Thought went up my mind today —
That I have had before —
But did not finish — some way back —
I could not fix the Year —

Nor where it went — nor why it came
The second time to me —
Nor definitely, what it was —
Have I the Art to say —

But somewhere — in my Soul — I know —
I've met the Thing before —
It just reminded me — 'twas all —
And came my way no more —

甘滴（NO.711）

汲取他人头脑中清新的甘滴
能使我雄赳赳
穿越过沙漠和荒野，好像携带着
封存了多年的好酒

或者——仿佛已经
获得了——骆驼的品质
难以想象这样一个头脑的
驱动力有多么了不起——

Strong Draughts of Their Refreshing Minds
To drink — enables Mine
Through Desert or the Wilderness
As bore it Sealed Wine —

To go elastic — Or as One
The Camel's trait — attained —
How powerful the Stimulus
Of an Hermetic Mind —

飞逝（NO.1714）

正在逝去的光能使我们
比凭借驻留的灯芯
看得更深锐，更清楚，
因为在其飞逝的当儿有什么东西
澄澈了视力
绚丽了光束。

By a departing light
We see acuter, quite,
Than by a wick that stays.
There's something in the flight
That clarifies the sight
And decks the rays.

难觅的知音

Rare Friend

我的朋友（NO.92）

我的朋友一定是只鸟——
因为它[①]能飞跑！
我的朋友不能永生，
因为它终会死掉！
它身上有倒刺，犹如蜜蜂！
啊，奇怪的朋友！
你真像是座迷宫！

My friend must be a Bird —
Because it flies!
Mortal, my friend must be,
Because it dies!
Barbs has it, like a Bee!
Ah, curious friend!
Thou puzzlest me!

① 这个它可能既指人也指自然万象。

迪姆和我（NO.196）

我们没有哭泣——迪姆和我，
因为我俩的心中充满了崇高——
我们只是扣上了门栓
不叫一个朋友进来——

随后我们用手掩住了我们
勇敢的面庞——
迪姆和我——不要恸哭——
因为有崇高在我们心中激荡——

我们——他和我——也不会屈尊
去把梦儿做——
我们只是阖上了眼睛
等着看到我们的终结——

迪姆——看到了房舍[①]
不过，噢，太高了！
于是——我们开始颤栗——迪姆和我——
为了安慰——我——

迪姆读起——一首赞美诗——
我们俩做着祈祷——
主啊，请宽恕，我和迪姆——
总是会迷失了道！

我们不久就会——死去——
牧师们说——
如果——我死了——迪姆也会——
如果他死了——我也不要活——

对此我们俩该做如何的安排——
迪姆——是那么的——羞怯？
主啊——请把我们两人同时带走——
“迪姆”——和我！

① 原文是“cottages”，这里指坟冢。

We don't cry — Tim and I,
We are far too grand —
But we bolt the door tight
To prevent a friend —

Then we hide our brave face
Deep in our hand —
Not to cry — Tim and I —
We are far too grand —

Nor to dream — he and me —
Do we condescend —
We just shut our brown eye
To see to the end —

Tim — see Cottages —
But, Oh, so high!
Then — we shake — Tim and I —
And lest I — cry —

Tim — reads a little Hymn —
And we both pray —
Please, Sir, I and Tim —
Always lost the way!

We must die — by and by —
Clergymen say —
Tim — shall — if I — do —
I — too — if he —

How shall we arrange it —
Tim — was — so — shy?
Take us simultaneous — Lord —
I — "Tim" — and Me!

寻觅（NO.842）

藏起来倾听他们的寻觅声，很开心！
可被找着了，更好，
如果是将遇良才，
恰如狐狸与猎狗能满足彼此的嗜好——

知道了不说出，固然好，
可知道了说出来，更好，
如果是你找到了难觅的知音
心有灵犀的相好——

Good to hide, and hear 'em hunt!

Better, to be found,

If one care to, that is,

The Fox fits the Hound —

Good to know, and not tell,

Best, to know and tell,

Can one find the rare Ear

Not too dull —

猜（NC.1653）

当我们走过房子时我们不免要想
是否有人已住在里面
头脑与头脑相遇时也在猜度
它们是否已被占满

As we pass Houses musing slow
If they be occupied
So minds pass minds
If they be occupied

朋友是一种高兴还是痛苦（NO.1199）

朋友是一种高兴还是痛苦？
如若财富能永远驻足
丰裕当然不错——

但是如果他们[1]的停留
只是为了羽翼丰满时飞走
那可是可悲的富足。

Are Friends Delight or Pain?
Could Bounty but remain
Riches were good —

But if they only stay
Ampler to fly away
Riches are sad.

① 指朋友也指财富。

素未谋面的人（NO.645）

从那些我们从未谋面的人的
逝世里感到一种损失——
这一点表达了在我们与这些死者的
灵魂之间有一种亲密的默契——

人们并不为陌生人的死哀悼——
可世间有许多永远不朽的人
在他们的死讯——传来时
我们便觉得失去了依凭——

这些于我们的思想至关重要的朋友——
在他们离去时仿佛带走了什么
我们不妨说，就好像是我们自己
蓦然间——失去了魂魄——

Bereavement in their death to feel
Whom We have never seen —
A Vital Kinsmanship import
Our Soul and theirs — between —

For Stranger — Strangers do not mourn —
There be Immortal friends
Whom Death see first — 'tis news of this
That paralyze Ourselves —

Who, vital only to Our Thought —
Such Presence bear away
In dying — 'tis as if Our Souls
Absconded — suddenly —

我不敢离开我的朋友（NO.205）

我不敢离开我的朋友，
因为——因为如果他死了
在我离去的时候——我会来不及——
抵达那颗渴望见到我的心儿——

如果我会使那双眼睛失望
那双一直在找寻——找寻——
在“看到”我——看到我之前——
不忍阖上的眼睛——

如果我会刺伤我朋友不渝的信念：
“我一定会来——我一定会来”——
所以他谛听着——谛听着——就在睡去的时候
仍然呼唤着我的名字——

如果是这样，我宁愿它[①]在这之前破灭——
因为于那时[②]破灭——于那时破灭——
就像第二天早晨的太阳一样于事无补——
既然已度不过今夜的——霜雪！

---

① 指朋友的那一信念。
② 指我刺伤它之后。

I should not dare to leave my friend,
Because — because if he should die
While I was gone — and I — too late —
Should reach the Heart that wanted me —

If I should disappoint the eyes
That hunted — hunted so — to see —
And could not bear to shut until
They "noticed" me — they noticed me —

If I should stab the patient faith
So sure I'd come — so sure I'd come —
It listening — listening — went to sleep —
Telling my tardy name —

My Heart would wish it broke before —
Since breaking then — since breaking then —
Were useless as next morning's sun —
Where midnight frosts — had lain!

世界显得飞尘扬扬（NO.715）

世界——显得飞尘扬扬
在我们歇下要离去时——
我们渴望有露水滋润——那时——
只觉荣誉功名——已枯燥无味——

旗帜会使一张于弥留之际的面庞蹙眉——
而由身旁一个朋友的手
举摇着的扇子
也能像甘霖凉爽了心头——

我会服侍在你身边
当你这般的又热又渴时——
我会为你取来——
海布拉河谷[①]的香粉和塞萨利的露水。

① 位于美国弗吉尼亚州。

The World — feels Dusty

When We stop to Die —

We want the Dew — then —

Honors — taste dry —

Flags — vex a Dying face —

But the least Fan

Stirred by a friend's Hand —

Cools — like the Rain —

Mine be the Ministry

When they Thirst comes —

And Hybla Balms —

Dews of Thessaly, to fetch —

我无须以言辞相对的朋友（NO.932）

与我最最要好的是那些
我无须以言词相对的朋友——
常常莅临小镇的星辰
永远不会觉得我粗鲁
虽然我不能回应它们那
来自天堂的召唤——
可是我的总是——充满虔诚的面庞
足以表达了我的敬慕。

My best Acquaintances are those
With Whom I spoke no Word —
The Stars that stated come to Town
Esteemed Me never rude
Although to their Celestial Call
I failed to make reply —
My constant — reverential Face
Sufficient Courtesy.

爱情的咏叹

Love Aria

爱情啊（NO.453）

爱情啊——你高高在上——
我不能将你攀登——
但是，如果是情侣一对——
谁敢说我们两个——
不会替换着——爬上钦博拉索山①——
像公爵一般——最终——与你并肩毗邻——

爱情啊——你深如海洋——
我不能把你横渡
不过，如果是两人情长
而不是一人孤独——
犹如划手，快艇——相默契——
谁敢说——我们俩不会把太阳追上？

爱情啊——你蒙着面纱——
只有少数人——看到你的面腮——
你或尔微笑或尔娇嗔或尔轻诉或尔消失
福祚里——缺少了你——会显得古怪——
上帝称你为——
与永恒同在——

① 厄瓜多尔中部的熄火山，为厄瓜多尔最高峰。

Love — thou art high —

I cannot climb thee —

But, were it Two —

Who know but we —

Taking turns — at the Chimborazo —

Ducal — at last — stand up by thee —

Love — thou are deep —

I cannot cross thee —

But, were there Two

Instead of One —

Rower, and Yacht — some sovereign Summer —

Who knows — but we'd reach the Sun?

Love — thou are Veiled —

A few — behold thee —

Smile — and alter — and prattle — and die —

Bliss — were an Oddity — without thee —

Nicknamed by God —

Eternity —

等待（NO.781）

等待一个小时——也会感到长——
如果爱情在你探不到的地方——
等再长的时间——也会觉得短——
如果爱情给予你报偿——

To wait an Hour — is long —
If Love be just beyond —
To wait Eternity — is short —
If Love reward the end —

距离（NO.1155）

距离——不是狐狸的领地
也不能凭借鸟儿的不懈飞翔
而缩短——距离一直存在
直至你自己，被人爱上。

Distance — is not the Realm of Fox
Nor by Relay of Bird
Abated — Distance is
Until thyself, Beloved.

我遇到了一个天使（NO.231）

上帝允准勤劳的天使们——
在下午的时候——下界游逛——
我遇到了一个——顿时忘掉了学友们——
我——整个身心——都扑到了——他身上——

日落时——上帝——将天使们——
还有我日夜想念的那一位召回——
在玩过皇冠之后
玉石显得多么乏味！

God permits industrious Angels —

Afternoons — to play —

I met one — forgot my Schoolmates —

All — for Him — straightway —

God calls home — the Angels — promptly —

At the Setting Sun —

I missed mine — how dreary — Marbles —

After playing Crown!

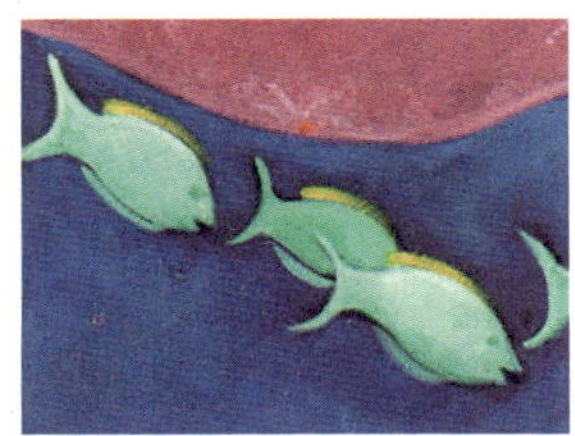

缅想（NO.815）

鉴赏方面的享受
那是一种享受
只要看上你一次，就是把
其他的琳琅满目

置之不顾，我已是一位美食家
我几乎不再记得
我希求过别的食粮
既然初次就给了我最好的——

冥想方面的享受
那也是一种享受
在心里宴飨你的面庞
这给我后来平淡朴素

之时日增添进一种奢华
它们[①]的餐桌上
只有一粒碎屑
那就是对你的缅想

① 指平淡无奇的时日。

The Luxury to apprehend
The Luxury 'twould be
To look at Thee a single time
An Epicure of Me

In whatsoever Presence makes
Till for a further Food
I scarcely recollect to starve
So first am I supplied —

The Luxury to meditate
The Luxury it was
To banguet on thy Countenance
A Sumptuousness bestows

On plainer Days, whose Table far
As Certainty can see
Is laden with a single Crumb
The Consciousness of Thee.

我总在爱你（NO.549）

我能证明给你看
我总在爱你
在我爱你之前——
我生活过得——没有生气——

我愿向你起誓——
我会一直爱你
爱情就是生活
生活里面有永恒存在——

这一点——亲爱的——如若你要怀疑——
那么除了痛苦
我再没有任何的东西
可向你表露——

That I did always love

I bring thee Proof

That till I loved

I never lived — Enough —

That I shall love alway —

I argue thee

That love is life —

And life hath Immortality —

This — dost thou doubt — Sweet —

Then have I

Nothing to show

But Calvary —

我愿我所是的正好合你的心（NO.738）

你有一天曾说过我——“伟大”——
“伟大”就“伟大”吧——如果这能使你高兴——
或者渺小——或者是在任何的水准上——
唔——我愿我所是的正好合你的心——

像牡鹿——那般高大——合你的意吗？
或是像一个弱小女子的——身材——
或是我所见过的其他任何
物种的体态？

说出你所喜欢的——一味的猜想多忧烦——
为了你我甘愿
同时是
犀牛——又是老鼠——

如果说——我是随从
或者皇后——能令你高兴
我就做他们
叫你称心——

You said that I "was Great" — one Day —
Then "Great" it be — if that please Thee —
Or Small — or any size at all —
Nay — I'm the size suit Thee —

Tall — like the Stag — would that?
Or lower — like the Wren —
Or other heights of Other Ones
I've seen?

Tell which — it's dull to guess —
And I must be Rhinoceros
Or Mouse —
At once — for Thee —

So say — if Queen it be —
Or Page — please Thee —
I'm that — or nought —
Or other thing — if other thing there be —
With just this Stipulus —
I suit Thee —

飞舞的蜜蜂（NO.869）

因为蜜蜂可以不受责备地嗡嗡
为了你我愿意变成一只蜜蜂
这样我便可以向你倾诉。

因为不知畏怯的鲜花可以
大胆地瞅着你，
我也愿意做一只花朵。

知更鸟儿也不必藏避
当你闯进它的巢穴时
所以请让我长出翅羽
或者变做花瓣，变做营营飞舞的蜜蜂，
或荆豆的花朵
啊，我就是这样全身心地将你爱慕。

Because the Bee may blameless hum
For Thee a Bee do I become
List even unto Me.

Because the Flowers unafraid
May lift a look on thine, a Maid
Alway a Flower would be.

Nor Robins, Robins need not hide
When Thou upon their Crypts intrude
So Wings bestow on Me
Or Petals, or a Dower of Buzz
That Bee to ride, or Flower of Furze
I that way worship Thee.

我是属于你的（NO.368）

除了你那儿——在别处消遣——我都受不了——
我知道了这一点——当有人用情把我缠绕
或许以为——我已疲惫——独自一人——
以为我受着——难以名状的痛苦的煎熬——

于是我变得——像公爵一般威严——
我是——属于你的——
你这港湾——对我这条小船——已经足矣——

尽管在涛涌的海里我们的小船会颠簸——
那也胜于——我独自在岸边停泊。
我们的小船——宁愿负重——荡在海里——
也不愿去到“芬芳的小岛”——
如那儿没有——你的作随——

How sick — to wait — in any place — but thine —
I knew last night — when someone tried to twine —
Thinking — perhaps — that I looked tired — or alone —
Or breaking — almost — with unspoken pain —

And I turned — ducal —
That right — was thine —
One port — suffices — for a Brig — like mine —

Ours be the tossing — wild though the sea —
Rather than a Mooring — unshared by thee.
Ours be the Cargo — unladed — here —
Rather than the "spicy isles —"
And thou — not there —

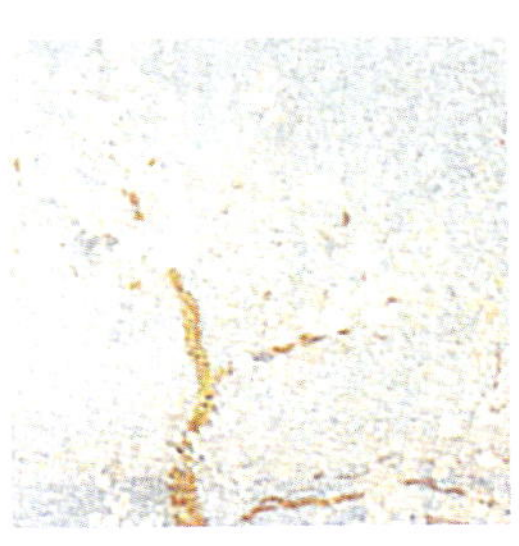

Selected Poems of
Emily Dickinson

唯有（NO.729）

改变！唯有当山峦改变了形状——
搪塞！唯有当太阳
怀疑地自问起他的光芒
是否是至高无尚——

餍足！唯有当水仙花儿
餍足了露水——
只有在那个时候——先生——
我才会——厌烦了你——

Alter! When the Hills do —
Falter! When the Sun
Question if His Glory
Be the Perfect One —

Surfeit! When the Daffodil
Doth of the Dew —
Even as Herself — O Friend —
I will of you —

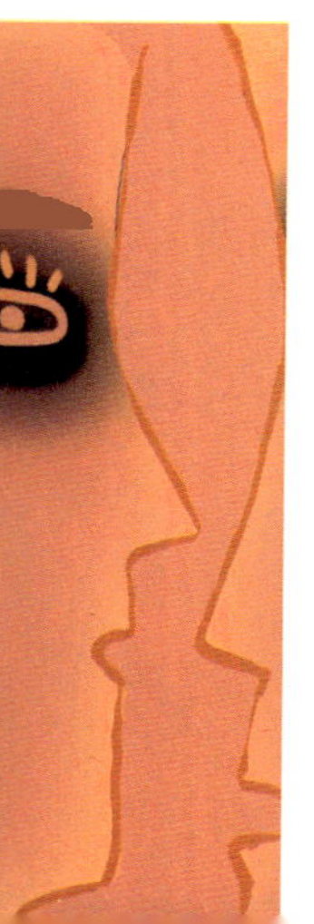

秋日（NO.129）

在我从未去过的国土——人们说
不朽的阿尔卑斯山峰俯瞰着一切——
它的山巅直刺苍穹——
它脚下的草地连着城池——

在它那亘古绵绵的山脚下
无数的雏菊轻轻地摇曳——
先生，这其中的哪一个是你，哪一个是我，
在这八月秋高气爽的时日？

In lands I never saw — they say
Immortal Alps look down —
Whose Bonnets touch the firmament —
Whose Sandals touch the town —

Meek at whose everlasting feet
A Myriad Daisy play —
Which, Sir, are you and which am I
Upon an August day?

我为什么爱你（NO.480）

“我为什么爱你”，先生？
因为——
风儿不要青草
回答——所以当风来到
草儿就折服屈腰

因为风儿晓得——你
不懂——
我也不懂——
我们的心智既然如是
还是让我们不作强求——

闪电——从来不曾问眼睛
在他经过时——它为什么闭紧——
因为他知道眼睛不会讲话——
而且有些原因话语里也
——包容不下——
哲人贤者——宁愿意会——

日出——先生——令我迷醉
因为他是日出——我能目睹——
同样的——原由——
我把你爱慕——

"Why do I love you", Sir?
Because —
The Wind does not require the Grass
To answer — Wherefore when He pass
She cannot keep Her place.

Because He knows — and
Do not You —
And We know not —
Enough for Us
The Wisdom it be so —

The Lightning — never asked an Eye
Wherefore it shut — when He was by —
Because He knows it cannot speak —
And reasons not contained —
— Of Talk —
There be — preferred by Daintier Folk —

The Sunrise — Sire — compelleth Me —
Because He's Sunrise — and I see —
Therefore — Then —
I love Thee —

将一切忘掉只为记起（NO.966）

将一切忘掉只为记起
一丁点儿——
将一切抛弃，只为了与一个
陌生的人相伴——

财富和地位的优越感
不如博得一个
默默的尊敬重要——
对此——谁能度测——

失去家园——对她[①]的缅怀和向往减弱——
自然万物——变小——
是否有太阳照耀——暴风雨肆虐——
这一切对我全不重要——

将我的命运——一颗胆怯的小卵石——
投进你的勇敢的大海[②]
如果我后悔了——亲爱的——你的行为——
会证明我这样做值——

① 指家园。
② 喻指陌生人的充满冒险的命运。

All forgot for recollecting
Just a paltry One —
All forsook, for just a Stranger's
New Accompanying —

Grace of Wealth, and Grace of Station
Less accounted than
An unknown Esteem possessing —
Estimate — Who can —

Home effaced — Her faces dwindled —
Nature — altered small —
Sun — if shone — or Storm — if shattered —
Overlooked I all —

Dropped — my fate — a timid Pebble —
In thy bolder Sea —
Prove — me — Sweet — if I regret it —
Prove Myself — of Thee —

实验（NO.1770）

“实验”一直为我们压阵到最后——
他陪伴我们寸步也不离
不给“金科玉律”
以可乘之机

Experiment escorts us last —
His pungent company
Will not allow an Axiom
An Opportunity

禁果（NO.1770）

禁果有一种通常的果树
会对它加以讥嘲的美味——
被本分锁缚着的豌豆是多么
娇艳诱人地躺在豆荚里——

Forbidden Fruit a flavor has
That lawful Orchards mocks —
How luscious lies within the Pod
The Pea that Duty locks —

我就会是一位新娘（NO.461）

黎明时——我就要成为一位妻子——
旭日啊——你可为我准备了一面旗帜？
在这一夜儿里，我还是一个姑娘，
可很快我就会是一位新娘——
那时——午夜，我已经走出了你
步入朝阳，步入胜利——

午夜——再见！我已听到他们[①]的召唤，
天使们已在大厅里争相露面——
我的未来正轻轻地爬上楼梯
慌乱中我把童年的祷告做起
庆幸我很快就不再是孩童——
永恒，我正在走近你，
主啊——以前——我曾见过你的面容！

① 指天使们。

A Wife — at daybreak I shall be —
Sunrise — Hast thou a Flag for me?
At Midnight, I am but a Maid,
How short it takes to make a Bride —
Then — Midnight, I have passed from thee
Unto the East, and Victory —

Midnight — Good Night! I hear them call,
The Angels bustle in the Hall —
Softly my Future climbs the Stair,
I fumble at my Childhood's prayer
So soon to be a Child no more —
Eternity, I'm coming — Sire,
Savior — I've seen the face — before!

触摸（NO.506）

他触摸了我，于是在他的默许下我生来
第一次体验了这样的一个日子，
我一点一点地伏上他的胸膛
它对我显得那么阔大
和平静，好像浩瀚的海洋
容纳了小溪来歇躺。

现在，我已经和从前不同，
仿佛我吮吸了最清醇的空气——
或是轻轻地触到了皇帝的衣裳——
我的徜徉了太久的脚儿——
我的吉卜赛人的面庞——
现在都变得温柔和淑雅——

进入这个港口，如果我可以，
丽贝卡，到耶路撒冷，
不会如此狂喜——
也没有波斯人，在她的圣坛上困惑
高举这受难的标志，
献给她庄严的太阳。

He touched me, so I live to know
That such a day, permitted so,
I groped upon his breast —
It was a boundless place to me
And silenced, as the awful sea
Puts minor streams to rest.

And now, I'm different from before,
As if I breathed superior air —
Or brushed a Royal Gown —
My feet, too, that had wandered so —
My Gypsy face — transfigured now —
To tenderer Renown —

Into this Port, if I might come,
Rebecca, to Jerusalem,
Would not so ravished turn —
Nor Persian, baffled at her shrine
Lift such a Crucifixial sign
To her imperial Sun.

红晕（NO.208）

一片红晕生动地浮上她的脸颊——
她紧身的胸衣在一起一伏——
她温文尔雅的言谈也变得结巴——
像是男人们喝醉了酒——

她做活计的手一时笨拙起来——
她的针儿也不听使唤——
是什么叫一个伶俐的姑娘现出难堪——
我很想解开这个谜团——

我终于发现——在我的对面
有个人脸上也有红晕一片——
对面的人儿——说话时
也似酩酊的醉汉——

像她的胸衣，这件背心也在和着
那一不朽的音律一伏一起——
直到这两个躁动的——小钟
跳上同一节拍，融为了一体。

The Rose did caper on her cheek —
Her Bodice rose and fell —
Her pretty speech — like drunken men —
Did stagger pitiful —

Her fingers fumbled at her work —
Her needle would not go —
What ailed so smart a little Maid —
It puzzled me to know —

Till opposite — I spied a cheek
That bore another Rose —
Just opposite — Another speech
That like the Drunkard goes —

A Vest that like her Bodice, danced —
To the immortal tune —
Till those two troubled — little Clocks
Ticked softly into one.

荒漠（NO.1754）

失去你——比赢得其他我所认识的
人的心都更觉温馨。
固然干旱是贫瘠，
可那时我曾有露水的滋润！

里海那儿有沙漠，
也有海域。
里海会不称其为里海，
如若没有了荒漠之地。

To lose thee — sweeter than to gain
All other hearts I knew.
'Tis true the drought is destitute,
But then, I had the dew!

The Caspian has its realms of sand,
Its other realm of sea.
Without the sterile perquisite,
No Caspian could be.

骰子（NO.886）

这些在我们的地平线上刚刚露面
便消失了
就像鸟群在快要飞到一个高度之前
突然没了影儿。

我们对它们的回顾
是一种欣怡，
而我们的预想和展望
却是一个疑虑 —— 一粒骰子 ——

These tested Our Horizon —

Then disappeared

As Birds before achieving

A Latitude.

Our Retrospection of Them

A fixed Delight,

But our Anticipation

A Dice — a Doubt —

我把自己藏在我的花束里（NO.903）

我把自己藏在我的花束里，
它正在你的花瓶里枯萎，
对此没有一点儿察觉的你，
几乎因为我而在感到孤寂。

I hide myself within my flower,
That fading from your Vase,
You, unsuspecting, feel for me —
Almost a loneliness.

激奋和陶醉感是一阵风儿（NO.1118）

激奋和陶醉感是一阵风儿
把我们从地面轻轻地举起
让我们到了另外一个处所
这地方我们用语言还无法表白——

它不把我们送回原地，而叫我们
稍后冷静地降落在
一处迷人的土地上
生命因此获得升华与光彩——

Exhilaration is the Breeze
That lifts us from the Ground
And leaves us in another place
Whose statement is not found —

Returns us not, but after time
We soberly descend
A little newer for the term
Upon Enchanted Ground —

无韵诗（NO.1150）

多少美好的计划很可能在
短短的一个下午泡了汤
而和它们密切相关的那些人
却也许对此毫无所知——
某个人没有失败或许
只是因为他偶尔
与其惯常的生活方式
偏离了分毫——
爱情不做这样的尝试
因为在爱巢的门外
定有些人想趁虚而入
一匹毫不叫人起疑心的马儿拴在屋外
正想看到恋人们陷于绝望

How many schemes may die

In one short Afternoon

Entirely unknown

To those they most concern —

The man that was not lost

Because by accident

He varied by a Ribbon's width

From his accustomed route —

The Love that would not try

Because beside the Door

It must be competitions

Some unsuspecting Horse was tied

Surveying his Despair

你忘了（NO.523）

亲爱的——你忘了——可是我每次记起
都是为了——我们两个人——
这样总和从来也不曾递减
由于你的超度红尘——

告诉我是否错了？怪罪我锱铢必较——
责备我手儿阔绰
为了你纵使我的手——变为乞丐的——
为你花费——我也欣然乞求更多——

让我成为富人——把每一个铜板都花在
这样一个美好的心灵上面——
让我沦为穷人——为使我看到你——亲爱的
平时——对我——掩饰的那一面——

Sweet — You forgot — but I remembered
Every time — for Two —
So that the Sum be never hindered
Through Decay of You —

Say if I erred? Accuse my Farthings —
Blame the little Hand
Happy it be for You — a Beggar's —
Seeking More — to spend —

Just to be Rich — to waste my Guineas
On so Best a Heart —
Just to be Poor — for Barefoot Vision
You — Sweet — Shut me out —

背誓者（NO.896）

背誓者是言语油滑穿着
硕大鞋子的蜜蜂
他总是把他的服侍给予
最新的达官贵人

他的追慕纯出于偶然
他的誓言只是言辞
就像微风持久而不停顿地
把结婚的预告宣布，他总是
把离婚的事儿提及。

Of Silken Speech and Specious Shoe
A Traitor is the Bee
His service to the newest Grace
Present continually

His Suit a chance
His Troth a Term
Protracted as the Breeze
Continual Ban propoundeth He
Continual Divorce.

离巢（NO.39）

那并不会令我惊奇——
我这样说——或这样想——
她迟早会翕动她的翮翼
将巢儿遗忘，

飞到更阔的树林——
在欣怡的枝条上筑巢，
向新一代的耳里
把上帝亘古的誓言轻祷——

这只是一只雏鸟——
那会怎样，如果
是我心中的真爱
远远地离开了我？

这只是一个故事——
那会怎样，如果
在人的心府里
真有这样的一个窝？

It did not surprise me —
So I said — or thought —
She will stir her pinions
And the nest forgot,

Traverse broader forests —
Build in gayer boughs,
Breathe in Ear more modern
God's old fashioned vows —

This was but a Birdling —
What and if it be
One within my bosom
Had departed me?

This was but a story —
What and if indeed
There were just such coffin
In the heart instead?

难忘（NO.47）

心儿！让我们把他忘记！
你和我——在今宵！
你可忘记他给予的温暖——
我将把那光儿忘掉！

在你忘记后，请告诉我
随后我会马上开始！
快！以免在你延误的当儿
我又把他想起！

Heart! We will forget him!

You and I — tonight!

You may forget the warmth he gave —

I will forget the light!

When you have done, pray tell me

That I may straight begin!

Haste! lest while you're lagging

I remember him!

你的素馨（NO.238）

戳破你的香剂袋儿——它的香味令你神怡——
把你的素馨裸放到——暴风雨里——
她将散发出最浓烈的香气——
或许——她会迷醉了你夏日的夜——

向在你心中筑巢的鸟儿——刺去——
噢，你可会听到她最后的唱词——
啁啾！“原谅我”——“比我好的会来”——啁啾！
“为他唱起颂歌——在我离去之时”！

Kill your Balm — and its Odors bless you —
Bare your Jessamine — to the storm —
And she will fling her maddest perfume —
Haply — your Summer night to Charm —

Stab the Bird — that built in your bosom —
Oh, could you catch her last Refrain —
Bubble! "forgive" — "Some better" — Bubble!
"Carol for Him — when I am gone"!

我们称过时间（NO.834）

在他到来之前我们称过时间！
它有时重有时轻。
当他离开之后，一种空虚感
是压倒了一切的负重。

Before He comes we weigh the Time!
'Tis Heavy and 'tis Light.
When He depart, an Emptiness
Is the prevailing Freight.

欢愉与悲伤

Joy and Sorrow

我能涉过悲伤·无韵诗（NO.252）

我能涉过悲伤——
涉过整个悲伤之河——
我已经习惯了它——
可是快乐的极轻微的一推搡
也会绊疼了我的脚——
我头重脚轻地——蹒跚
足下的每块卵石都使我紧张
因为这快乐是我未尝过的新酒——
仅此而已！

力量只是痛苦的——
凝聚，备受磨炼，
直到——能以负重——
给巨人们——以止痛剂——
他们会像常人一样萎顿——
给予其希玛尔勒[①]——
他们却能将他——抬起！

① 其人不详，可能是神话传说中的高大无比的巨人。

I can wade Grief —
Whole Pools of it —
I'm used to that —
But the least push of Joy
Breaks up my feet —
And I tip — drunken —
Let no Pebble — smile —
'Twas the New Liquor —
That was all!

Power is only Pain —
Stranded, thro' Discipline,
Till Weights — will hang —
Give Balm — to Giants —
And they'll wilt, like Men —
Give Himmaleh —
They'll Carry — Him!

对悲伤进行回味（NO.660）

这是有益的——对悲伤进行回味——
去重新熬过那一日——
那一我们认为是埋葬了我们——
心中所有欢乐的日子——

去回顾快长的青草如何
一点点地——蔓延过来——
直到悲哀挥手与夏日——告别
我们再也看不到它[①]的墓石。

虽然你今天所受的痛苦
更为巨大——就像大海
远远超过注入到它里面的水滴——
可是它们都同样——是水——

① 指悲哀。

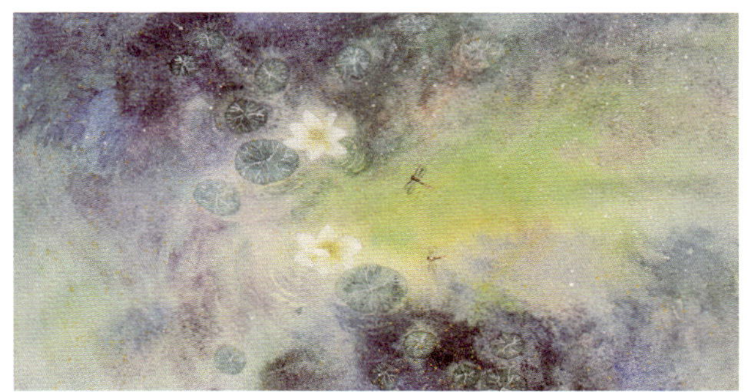

Tis good — the looking back on Grief —
To re-endure a Day —
We thought the Mighty Funeral —
Of All Conceived Joy —

To recollect how Busy Grass
Did meddle — one by one —
Till all the Grief with Summer — waved
And none could see the stone.

And though the Woe you have Today
Be larger — As the Sea
Exceeds its Unremembered Drop —
They're Water — equally —

我突然把它想念（NO.743）

从南方飞回来的鸟儿向我——
报道着快讯——
这曾给我多大的快感，我的传书的飞雁——
可是今天我却似乎——听而不闻——

含羞初绽的花蕾——向我招着手儿
我把房门关牢——
鲜花，去找蜜蜂吧——我说——
请不要再把我——搅扰——

夏日的妩媚，要我对她垂青——.
离我远一点——你这艳丽——
我的心儿——已完全把我
眺望的心思熄灭——

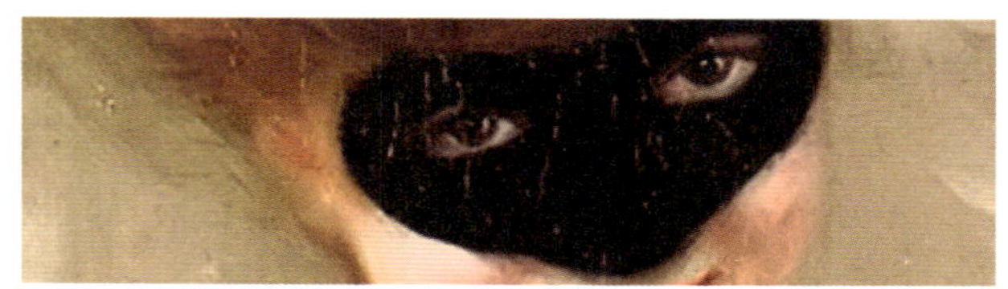

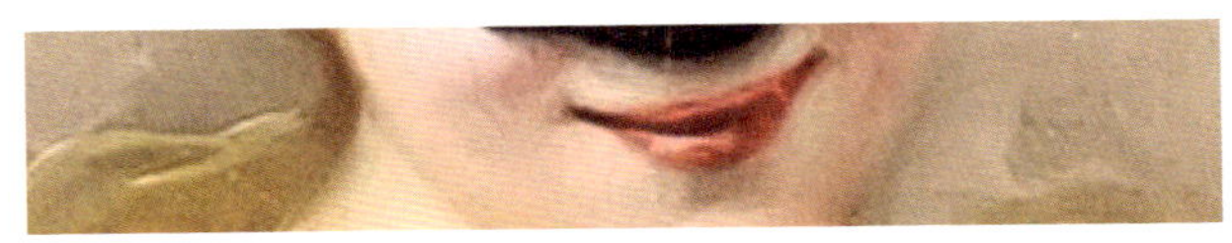

临了，一个像我一样的人，
在离群索居，郁郁寡欢——
沉湎在她的悲戚之中——此时
我突然把她想念——

她接纳了我，因为我也经受了悲伤——
我对她默默无语——
我哀伤的标志——是我戴着的黑纱——
她的——是她死去的亲属——

从此以后——我们——住在了一起——
我从未问起过她的伤心事——
彼此心照不宣的同情
是我们之间的默契

The Birds reported from the South —
A News express to Me —
A spicy Charge, My little Posts —
But I am deaf — Today —

The Flowers — appealed — a timid Throng —
I reinforced the Door —
Go blossom for the Bees — I said —
And trouble Me — no More —

The Summer Grace, for Notice strove —
Remote — Her best Array —
The Heart — to stimulate the Eye
Refused too utterly —

At length, a Mourner, like Myself,
She drew away austere —
Her frosts to ponder — then it was
I recollected Her —

She suffered Me, for I had mourned —
I offered Her no word —
My Witness — was the Crape I bore —
Her — Witness — was Her Dead —

Thenceforward — We — together dwelt —
I never questioned Her —
Our Contract
A Wiser Sympathy

悲伤沉默不语（NO.793）

悲伤是只老鼠——
选择心府的内壁
作他的避羞处——
把一切探寻阻止——

悲伤是个小偷——极易受到惊吓——
竖着耳朵——倾听漫漫黑暗
给他的报导——
正是这黑暗使他敢于——出壳——

悲伤是个变戏法的——在台上毫无惧色——
免得他一畏缩——叫明眼的
瞥视到他的创伤——一个——哦——或三个——
悲伤是个美食家——懂得节制他的奢华——

悲伤沉默无语——让他开口——
还不如把他在广场上焚烧——
他的骨灰——也许会说出——
如若它们[①]拒绝——那他怎么会被知晓呢——
既然什么折磨也不能诱出音节一个。

① 指他的骨灰。

Grief is a Mouse —
And chooses Wainscot in the Breast
For His Shy House —
And baffles quest —

Grief is a Thief — quick startled —
Pricks His Ear — report to hear
Of that Vast Dark —
That swept His Being — back —

Grief is a Juggler — boldest at the Play —
Lest if He flinch — the eye that way
Pounce on His Bruises — One — say — or Three —
Grief is a Gourmand — spare His luxury —

Best Grief is Tongueless — before He'll tell —
Burn Him in the Public Square —
His Ashes — will
Possibly — if they refuse — How then know —
Since a Rack couldn't coax a syllable — now.

儿时的绝望（NO.1738）

受着时间之流的冲刷
那一威胁着我们童年的城堡
暗伤了我们童年岁月的痛苦
现在似乎已全无了棱角。

被更凄然的悲伤煎熬着
我们妒忌起儿时的绝望
那一摧毁了我们童年的王国
可却易于修复的绝望。

Softened by Time's consummate plush,
How sleek the woe appears
That threatened childhood's citadel
And undermined the years.

Bisected now, by bleaker griefs,
We envy the despair
That devastated childhood's realm,
So easy to repair.

这儿有一种痛苦（NO.599）

这儿有一种痛苦——是那么彻底——
它把物质整个儿吞噬——
然后用恍惚掩盖起深渊——
这样记忆便可在它[①]的周围
迈起步子——甚至——踏于其上——
就像一个人在晕眩时——
能安然行走于危境——在那里只要一睁眼
就会将他摔得——粉碎。

There is a pain — so utter —
It swallows substance up —
Then covers the Abyss with Trance —
So Memory can step
Around — across — upon it —
As one within a Swoon —
Goes safely — where an open eye —
Would drop Him — Bone by Bone.

---

① 指深渊。

我喜欢痛苦的表情（NO.241）

我喜欢痛苦的表情，
因为我知道它是真实的——
人们并不假装痉挛，
或是把巨痛遮掩——

目光只有一次变得呆滞——那便是死亡——
由刺心窝的痛楚
在额头沁出的汗珠
不可能被装出。

I like a look of Agony,
Because I know it's true —
Men do not sham Convulsion,
Nor simulate, a Throe —

The Eyes glaze once — and that is Death —
Impossible to feign
The Beads upon the Forehead
By homely Anguish strung.

它有空白点（NO.650）

痛苦的一个特征是——它有空白点——
它不能记起
它始于何时——或者是否有一个
时间它不曾存在——

它没有未来——只有它自己
它把无限囊括
过去的它——启迪着人们去感知
新的时期的痛苦。

Pain — has an Element of Blank —
It cannot recollect
When it begun — or if there were
A time when it was not —

It has no Future — but itself —
Its Infinite contain
Its Past — enlightened to perceive
New Periods — of Pain.

经受（NO.799）

“失望”的裨益需通过经受了
失望——才能获得——
要想从逆境那儿得到助益
须经受了逆境的折磨——

受难的价值宛如
死的价值只有
品尝了才知道——

从任何救世主的口中

得知——都不如——
我们自己的亲自参与——
痛苦会显得不疼不痒
在降至我们身上之前——

Despair's advantage is achieved
By suffering — Despair —
To be assisted of Reverse
One must Reverse have bore —

The Worthiness of Suffering like
The Worthiness of Death
Is ascertained by tasting —

As can no other Mouth

Of Savors — make us conscious —
As did ourselves partake —
Affliction feels impalpable
Until Ourselves are struck —

原谅（NO.538）

确实——他们关我在冷室里——
不过——他们自己那时很温暖
不可能体尝了冷的滋味——
所以主呵——请原谅了——他们——

不要让对我的这一不公阻碍了
他们得到别人的尊重——
天堂不可能赐给——那些
被爱他们的人所责骂的人——

他们给予的伤害——是短暂的——而且
承受了这一伤害的我——已的确
原谅了他们——即便我自己——
或是别人——还没有原谅我——

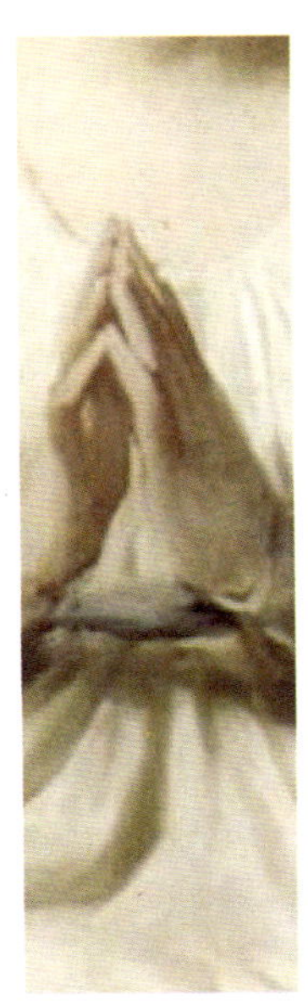

'Tis true — They shut me in the Cold —
But then — Themselves were warm
And could not know the feeling 'twas —
Forget it — Lord — of Them —

Let not my Witness hinder Them
In Heavenly esteem —
No Paradise could be — Conferred
Through Their beloved Blame —

The Harm They did — was short — And since
Myself — who bore it — do —
Forgive Them — Even as Myself —
Or else — forgive not me —

迷途的我（NO.953）

一扇临街的门刚好打开——
迷途的我——正巧走过——
片刻的温暖从里面泄出——
还有富足——和天伦之乐。

门霎那间便关上了——我——
迷途的我——正在走过——
这一痛苦的——对比——使我倍感——
迷失——和萧瑟——

A Door just opened on a street —
I — lost — was passing by —
An instant's Width of Warmth disclosed —
And Wealth — and Company.

The Door as instant shut — And I —
I — lost — was passing by —
Lost doubly — but by contrast — most —
Informing — misery —

8

时间在前进（NO.1121）

时间的确在向前进——
我欣然地告诉那些正在受苦的人——
他们将活过苦难——
生活将充满阳光——
对此他们现在并不相信——

Time does go on —
I tell it gay to those who suffer now —
They shall survive —
There is a sun —
They don't believe it now —

时间可以平息一切（NO.686）

人们说“时间可以平息一切”——
其实时间从不曾将什么平息——
一种实在的痛苦，伴随岁月的增长
只会加强恰如有痼疾的人的机体——

时间是一种对有无弊病的检验——
而不是一副良方——
如果此点可以证实，那么也可以证实
不曾有任何弊端能把时间欺诓——

They say that "Time assuages" —
Time never did assuage —
An actual suffering strengthens
As Sinews do, with age —

Time is a Test of Trouble —
But not a Remedy —
If such it prove, it prove too
There was no Malady —

内里的损伤（NO.1123）

一个大的希望落空
你听不到响声
致命的损伤是在内里
哦，狡猾的厄运来得悄无声息
不让一个见证人入内

心灵能承受巨大的负载
能面对危险恐怖的情况
尽管似乎常常沉浸在
海里，可在陆地上

却不许有半点的伤痛露出
直至伤口变得如此之阔
我的生命都入到了它里面
在顶盖的闭合处

还会有一些罅隙
叫阳光射进
直至勤谨的木匠
把盖子牢牢地钉紧——

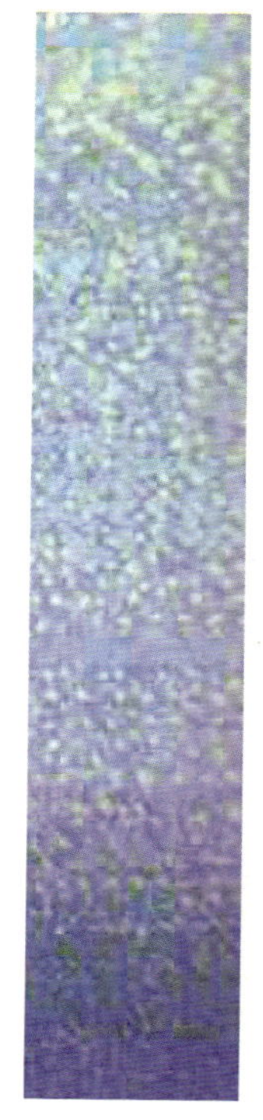

A great Hope fell
You heard no noise
The Ruin was within
Oh cunning wreck that told no tale
And let no Witness in

The mind was built for mighty Freight
For dread occasion planned
How often foundering at Sea
Ostensibly, on Land

A not admitting of the wound
Until it grew so wide
That all my Life had entered it
And there were troughs beside

A closing of the simple lid
That opened to the sun
Until the tender Carpenter
Perpetual nail it down —

幸福（NO.1057）

我有一种天天享有的幸福
我并没有把它放在心上
直到有一天我突然察觉到它的涌动——
以后伴随着我的追慕它日见成长

直到跨过一个高度
错过了我的视线
大到无法再用我惯常的标准
对它进行估算。

I had a daily Bliss

I half indifferent viewed

Till sudden I perceived it stir —

It grew as I pursued

Till when around a Height

It wasted from my sight

Increased beyond my utmost scope

I learned to estimate.

心语（NO.1750）

快乐的人们说出的话语
像轻快的小曲
而缄默的人们的心语
更是美妙无比——

The words the happy say
Are paltry melody
But those the silent feel
Are beautiful —

无处安身的欢欣（NO.1186）

晨光太短暂

良宵也无多

所以对天降的欢欣

没有一个处所

不愿对之接受，

免得它无处安身

再悄然溜走。

Too few the mornings be,

Too scant the nights.

No lodging can be had

For the delights

That come to earth to stay,

But no apartment find

And ride away.

销魂的代价（NO.125）

为每一个极乐时刻的到来
我们须付出痛苦的代价
其剧烈和震撼的程度
与销魂的快乐相当。

为这种幸福时刻的来至
我们须日积月累
锱铢必较地拼争——
需流去多少的眼泪和汗水！

For each ecstatic instant
We must an anguish pay
In keen and quivering ration
To the ecstasy.

For each beloved hour
Sharp pittances of years —
Bitter contested farthings —
And Coffers heaped with Tears!

我这短短的一生（NO.178）

我仔细地审视我的短短的一生——
我把犹如昙花会很快消褪的部分簸掉
留下永驻的，直到这一筛选
乏累得我快要睡着。

我把后者放进谷仓——
而扇跑了前者。
一个冬天的早晨我去查看
噢——我那无价的收获[①]

不在搁架上——
也没在“大梁”上悬搁——
从一个富足的农夫——
我一下子变成一个愤世嫉俗者。

我很想发现出
这到底是贼人所为——
还是风儿把它们吹跑——
还是上帝在作祟！

于是我开始翻箱倒柜！
你们怎么了，吾之精华？
你们还在这由吾爱提供给
你们的小小谷仓里吗？

① 原文是“hay”是干草之意，这里指收获。

I cautious, scanned my little life —
I winnowed what would fade
From what would last till Heads like mine
Should be a-dreaming laid.

I put the latter in a Barn —
The former, blew away.
I went one winter morning
And lo - my priceless Hay

Was not upon the "Scaffold" —
Was not upon the "Beam" —
And from a thriving Farmer —
A Cynic, I became.

Whether a Thief did it —
Whether it was the wind —
Whether Deity's guiltless —
My business is, to find!

So I begin to ransack!
How is it Hearts, with Thee?
Art thou within the little Barn
Love provided Thee?

终结之力（NO.1196）

记想着惯常的一切都可能会停止
就会变习以为常为一种刺激——
终结的力量是一种
特别的恩惠——

反省之箭在修复
那一随巨痛
而去的终结之力时
啊，便变得更加迷人——

To make Routine a Stimulus
Remember it can cease —
Capacity to Terminate
Is a Specific Grace —

Of Retrospect the Arrow
That power to repair
Departed with the Torment
Become, alas, more fair —

痛苦却没有一根能飞的羽毛（NO.1774）

极乐的时日把自己消融
未留下任何痕迹——
痛苦却没有一根能飞的羽毛
或是负重太过飞不起来——

Too happy Time dissolves itself
And leaves no remnant by —
'Tis Anguish not a Feather hath
Or too much weight to fly —

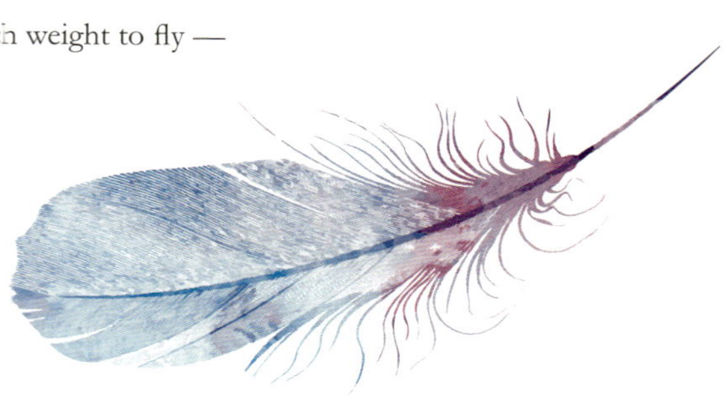

剩下的那一半时光（NO.1715）

看看夏日的钟表
只留下了一半的时光。
得知了这一事实我惊了一跳——
我再也不愿去看它。
剩下的那一半快乐光阴
要比前面一半过得快得多。
对这一我不敢去了解的真相
我讥嘲似的捂住了嘴不予说出。

Consulting summer's clock,
But half the hours remain.
I ascertain it with a shock —
I shall not look again.
The second half of joy
Is shorter than the first.
The truth I do not dare to know
I muffle with a jest.

心灵中美好的疑问（NO.1413）

心灵中所存的美好的疑问
有时候确信——有时候不信——
恰如阵阵的芳香受大雪的阻隔
在大气中的来回飘动——

先是邀来然后又滞留真理
免得叫肯定趋于枯萎
与那一由担心所引起的使人陶然的
痛苦和痴迷相比[①]——

① 这里指在肯定和担心所引起的种种情形之间的对比。

Sweet Skepticism of the Heart —
That knows — and does not know —
And tosses like a Fleet of Balm —
Affronted by the snow —

Invites and then retards the Truth
Lest Certainty be sere
Compared with the delicious throe
Of transport thrilled with Fear —

啊未来（NO.1631）

啊未来！你是神秘的平静
是藏匿着的痛苦——
可有一条幽幽的曲径
通向远离你的处所——
可有一条迂回盘绕的路被精明
狡黠的人找到
从而把你阻拦在路上——
叫你无法回到你的窝巢——

Oh Future! thou secreted peace
Or subterranean woe —
Is there no wandering route of grace
That leads away from thee —
No circuit sage of all the course
Descried by cunning Men
To balk thee of thy sacred Prey —
Advancing to thy Den —

漂泊（NO.1382）

在许多名不见经传的地方
我们感到了一种欢欣——
它[①]没有定名，可却像造化
或神明一样的真诚——

它来，来得悄无声息，——
逝去时——也是同样——
不过却留下一种无尽的难以
名状的惆怅——

我们不能——凭着搜寻玷污到它
因为它没有家——
曾体验了这一快乐的我们也没有了家
从此开始了漂泊生涯。

① 指欢欣。

In many and reportless places
We feel a Joy —
Reportless, also, but sincere as Nature
Or Deity —

It comes, without a consternation —
Dissolves — the same —
But leaves a sumptuous Destitution —
Without a Name —

Profane it by a search — we cannot
It has no home —
Nor we who having once inhaled it —
Thereafter roam.

慧眼（NO.435）

许多的疯狂里有着神圣的意义——
对善识的慧眼——
许多的理性——却是地道的疯狂——
在这里——如在一切其他的场合一样
总是大多数人的意见占了上风——
同意他们——你就是理智健全——
反对他们——你便是大逆不道——
需要戴上锁链——

Much Madness is divinest Sense —
To a discerning Eye —
Much Sense — the starkest Madness —
'Tis the Majority
In this, as All, prevail —
Assent — and you are sane —
Demur — you're straightway dangerous —
And handled with a Chain —

希望是精灵（NO.254）

“希望”是长着羽翼的精灵——
它栖息在心灵里——
唱着没有歌词的曲调——
从来没有过一刻儿——停止——

在飙风里——它听着——最可亲——
那样的暴风雨一定很凄苦——
如果这小鸟的诸般温馨
在寒冷里全被祛除——

在严寒料峭的国土，在天涯海角——
我都听到它的歌唱——
然而，不管多艰苦的环境，
它都不要我对它——犒赏。

"Hope" is the thing with feathers —
That perches in the soul —
And sings the tune without the words —
And never stops — at all —

And sweetest — in the Gale — is heard —
And sore must be the storm —
That could abash the little Bird
That kept so many warm —

I've heard it in the chillest land —
And on the strangest Sea —
Yet, never, in Extremity,
It asked a crumb — of Me.

乏味（NO.782）

缺乏生气的愉悦
与快乐不同——
就像冰霜不同于露水——
虽然它们有着相同的成分——

它们一个——使花儿欢欣
一个叫花儿憎厌——
最好的蜂蜜——如果凝结了——
也会对蜜蜂——毫无价值可言——

There is an arid Pleasure —
As different from Joy —
As Frost is different from Dew —
Like element — are they —

Yet one — rejoices Flowers —
And one — the Flowers abhor —
The finest Honey — curdled —
Is worthless — to the Bee —

不要有一点儿声响（NO.1185）

一只小狗高兴地摇晃着尾巴
再也不知道有别的愉快
由这条小狗我想到
了一个男孩

没有任何世俗的原因
他整天价的嬉戏快乐
只因为他是一个孩童
我真诚地这般揣测

蜷缩在隅角里的猫
忘掉了她的光荣
捕鼠对她已成为过去
她的这种百无聊赖的命运

叫我想起一个课堂
那儿既不做游戏又没有偷悦
只是一味地要求孩子们
不要有“一点儿的声响”发出

A little Dog that wags his tail
And knows no other joy
Of such a little Dog am I
Reminded by a Boy

Who gambols all the living Day
Without an earthly cause
Because he is a little Boy
I honestly suppose —

The Cat that in the Corner dwells
Her martial Day forgot
The Mouse but a Tradition now
Of her desireless Lot

Another class remind me
Who neither please nor play
But not to make a "bit of noise"
Beseech each little Boy —

一点一点到来的美好（NO.1726）

如果我将来要忍受的悲痛
都在今天到来，
我相信我会非常的高兴
以至它们全都会笑着跑开。

如果我将来享有的快乐
都在今天来到，
它们就不会像现在这样
一点一点到来的美好。

If all the griefs I am to have
Would only come today,
I am so happy I believe
They'd laugh and run away.

If all the joys I am to have
Would only come today,
They could not be so big as this
That happens to me now.

甜美的时光（NO.1734）

噢，甜美的时光，
我还未曾体味过你的力量，
我现在持有的禀赋
还不配荣享
这最美好的时光，
所以先不要给予我

Oh, honey of an hour,
I never knew thy power,
Prohibit me
Till my minutest dower,
My unfrequented flower,
Deserving be.

新幕（NO.839）

快结束吧！
我休憩的日子！
今天开始了充满光明的时期！
它不会有闪失
就如太阳和四季的轮回。

古老的优美品质，新颖的主题——
东方啊，你源自远古，
可是在你那紫金色的天幕上
每一个黎明，都是新的一幕。

Always Mine!
No more Vacation!
Term of Light this Day begun!
Failless as the fair rotation
Of the Seasons and the Sun.

Old the Grace, but new the Subjects —
Old, indeed, the East,
Yet upon His Purple Programme
Every Dawn, is first.

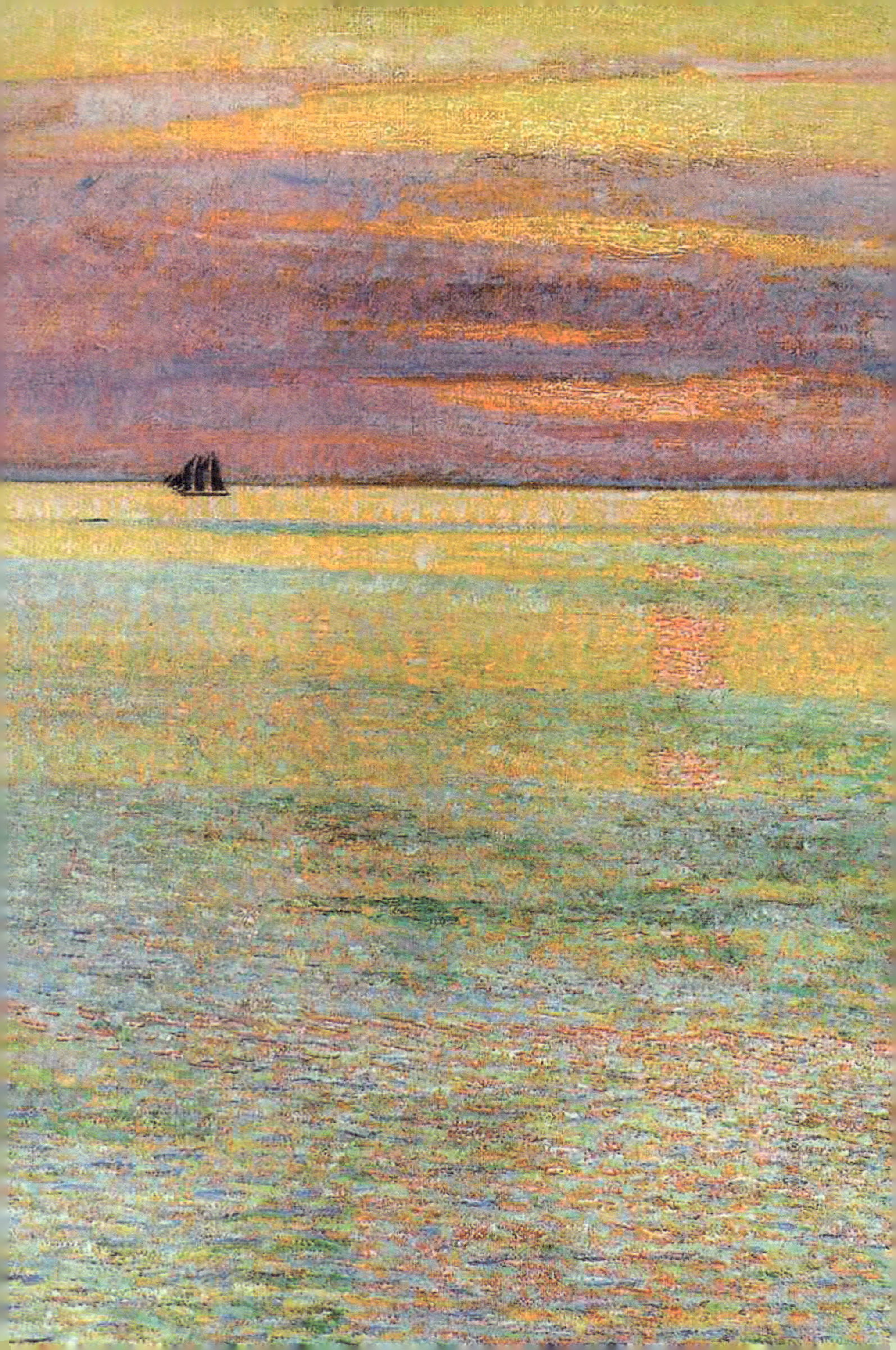

静水流深
Still Water

童心（NO.637）

孩童的信心还不曾被玷污——
它浑然一体——犹如他的理念——
它阔大无边——犹如日出时满天的朝辉
在他天真无瑕的眼睛里——
从来没有过怀疑的阴影——
他嘲笑——小心谨慎——
相信所有的欺哄
唯独不信天堂——

他对世界充满好奇——
认为他的制统的权力
充溢宇宙，无边无沿——
恺撒大帝——跟他相比——
也会显得卑微——
他虽说是没有疆域的帝王
没有臣民的统治者，
却能够征服一切——

随着年事的增长
他美好的憧憬
一个个地被
多刺的现实击中
像有些人，而不是
像帝王们——那样——
他开始——用感伤的眼光
去看未来——

The Child's faith is new—

Whole—like His Principle—

Wide—like the Sunrise

On fresh Eyes—

Never had a Doubt—

Laughs—at a Scruple—

Believes all sham

But Paradise—

Credits the World—

Deems His Dominion

Broadest of Sovereignties—

And Caesar—mean—

In the Comparison—

Baseless Emperor—

Ruler of Nought—

Yet swaying all—

Grown bye and bye

To hold mistaken

His pretty estimates

Of Prickly Things

He gains the skill

Sorrowful—as certain—

Men—to anticipate

Instead of Kings—

我有一个国王（NO.103）

我有一个国王，他缄默无语——
因此——无主地——我捱过
白天那平和的时光——
晚上入睡，如果偶尔在梦中，
我窥入被白天关闭的王城
心里便有了些许的欢畅。

如果是这样——当早晨来到——
就好像有千百只战鼓在敲
它们震响在我的睡枕，
呐喊声充斥着我孩童似的天空，
从我灵魂的尖顶
不断传出宣告“胜利”的钟声！

如果不是这样——我就会连
果园里小鸟的啼声也听不见，
我这一天就不做“主噢，
你的旨意我会照办”的祈祷
因为我的意愿在行着相反的道，
我的祷告会与主的相拗！

I have a King, who does not speak —
So — wondering — thro' the hours meek
I trudge the day away —
Half glad when it is night, and sleep,
If, haply, thro' a dream, to peep
In parlors, shut by day.

And if I do — when morning comes —
It is as if a hundred drums
Did round my pillow roll,
And shouts fill all my Childish sky,
And Bells keep saying "Victory"
From steeples in my soul!

And if I don't — the little Bird
Within the Orchard, is not heard,
And I omit to pray
"Father, thy will be done" today
For my will goes the other way,
And it were perjury!

忏悔（NO.744）

忏悔——是醒着的——记忆——
霎时间一切都活跃起来——
过去在一幕幕地展现——
于窗口——于门扉

过去——在灵魂面前立定
由火柴儿照亮——
以利对它的审视——
以帮助把信心发扬光大——

忏悔无药可医——对此病
上帝甚至也——无能为力——
因为这正是上帝的旨意——
对地狱也适宜——

Remorse — is Memory — awake —
Her Parties all astir —
A Presence of Departed Acts —
At window — and at Door —

Its Past — set down before the Soul
And lighted with a Match —
Perusal — to facilitate —
And help Belief to stretch —

Remorse is cureless — the Disease
Not even God — can heal —
For 'tis His institution — and
The Adequate of Hell —

羞愧（NO.1412）

羞愧是一条粉红色的围巾
我们用它将我们的灵魂包起
使它[①]免于受眼睛的侵扰——
大自然的纱帷
是无望的自然撒下
当她被推逼到一个
与她的真诚相悖的境地——
羞愧是一种神圣的色泽。

① 指灵魂。

Shame is the shawl of Pink
In which we wrap the Soul
To keep it from infesting Eyes —
The elemental Veil
Which helpless Nature drops
When pushed upon a scene
Repugnant to her probity —
Shame is the tint divine.

距离（NO.439）

一个饥肠辘辘的人对食物
会过分的青睐——
他立在远处——叹息——于是乎变得无望——
于是乎——一切对他都是珍馐美味——

享用之后——的确——难耐的饥饿消失了——
可是却也向我们证明
那扑鼻的香味也随之
消散了——是距离的作用——
造出诱人的美味——

Undue Significance a starving man attaches
To Food —
Far off — He sighs — and therefore — Hopeless —
And therefore — Good —

Partaken — it relieves — indeed —
But proves us
That Spices fly
In the Receipt — It was the Distance —
Was Savory —

崇仰（NO.1429）

我们不去看，是因为我们太崇仰她的容颜
以免眼睛自己无法去掉羞辱
从而玷污了我们对她的仰慕

We shun because we prize her Face
Lest sight's ineffable disgrace
Our Adoration stain

无限（NO.1309）

无限被认为是——
突然而至的宾客——
可是这个从未离开过的浩瀚[①]
又如何能到来呢？

The Infinite a sudden Guest
Has been assumed to be —
But how can that stupendous come
Which never went away?

---

① 喻指无限

无欲无求（NO.779）

不带任何欲求的付出——
我想，最最温馨——
因为这种付出没有看得见的
利益支撑——求报偿的劳动——

有将来的所得为动力——
有一个吸引人的目的——
没有理想在胸的勤勉
恐怕就不存在——

The Service without Hope —
Is tenderest, I think —
Because 'tis unsustained
By stint — Rewarded Work —

Has impetus of Gain —
And impetus of Goal —
There is no Diligence like that
That knows not an Until —

淑雅（NO.810）

她的淑雅是她拥有的一切——
而就这一点，她也丝毫不愿张扬——
为此必须有一种本领，去对其认可，
另一种本领，去颂扬。

Her Grace is all she has —
And that, so least displays —
One Art to recognize, must be,
Another Art, to praise.

秘密（NO.381）

秘密一旦说出——
它就不再是个——秘密——
秘密——埋在心底
只能是吓坏了守密者自己——

即便如此——担惊受怕地守着秘密
还是要——
胜于你把它泄露了——出去——

A Secret told —

Ceases to be a Secret — then —

A Secret — kept —

That — can appal but One —

Better of it — continual be afraid —

Than it —

And Whom you told it to — beside —

诗人（NO.448）

这样的一位就是诗人——如果他能
从平常的意义中
提取出不寻常的意蕴——
从我们门前凋零

常见的花卉里
把巨量的玫瑰油提炼——
有时我们禁不住会问是不是
我们自己——做出了这样的发现——

诗人——是启迪者——
于他描绘的画面里——
我们看到了——通过鲜明的对比——
自己的匮乏和无知——

他没有一点儿的占有欲
抢劫——并不能损害到
他自己——在他看——财富——
只是时间的——外壳——

This was a Poet — It is That
Distills amazing sense
From ordinary Meanings —
And Attar so immense

From the familiar species
That perished by the Door —
We wonder it was not Ourselves
Arrested it — before —

Of Pictures, the Discloser —
The Poet — it is He —
Entitles Us — by Contrast —
To ceaseless Poverty —

Of portion — so unconscious —
The Robbing — could not harm —
Himself — to Him — a Fortune —
Exterior — to Time —

我宁愿（NO.505）

我不愿——绘画——
我宁愿自己是幅画
能甜甜地品味
画帙的——出神入化——
揣摩画工的手指有如何的感受
它的——鬼斧神工的——挥洒——
引发豪情无限——
绝望的浪潮——无涯——

我不愿意说个没完没了——
我宁愿自己做短号一只
袅袅的余音轻柔地绕梁——
溢出屋外，飘升不止——
荡漾在村舍，荡漾在蓝天——
宛如是被一个号嘴
吹入天空的气球——
宛如码头上浮桥的漂摆——

我也不愿做一个诗人
使用耳朵——我觉得更好——
被陶醉——慵倦——满足——
倾慕和景仰是我的嗜好。
这样的特权实在糟糕
有天赋又如何，
如果我的艺术用它那电触似的旋律
把我惊得目瞪口呆！

I would not paint — a picture —
I'd rather be the One
Its bright impossibility
To dwell — delicious — on —
And wonder how the fingers feel
Whose rare — celestial — stir —
Evokes so sweet a Torment —
Such sumptuous — Despair —

I would not talk, like Cornets —
I'd rather be the One
Raised softly to the Ceilings —
And out, and easy on —
Through Villages of Ether —
Myself endued Balloon
By but a lip of Metal —
The pier to my Pontoon —

Nor would I be a Poet —

It's finer — own the Ear —

Enamored — impotent — content —

The License to revere,

A privilege so awful

What would the Dower be,

Had I the Art to stun myself

With Bolts of Melody!

真理（NO.836）

真理——像上帝一样古老——
是上帝的双重身份
将像上帝一样延长到久远
永与上帝共存——
真理将消亡，在上帝
从宇宙之大厦中
被带走了的那一日，到那时
它便成了无生命的种

Truth — is as old as God —
His Twin identity
And will endure as long as He
A Co-Eternity —
And perish on the Day
Himself is borne away
From Mansion of the Universe
A lifeless Deity.

要是和万一（NO.1161）

信任在修正着她[1]的“要是和万一”——

因为已进来的是幻觉，“而不是你。”

rust adjust her "Peradventure" —

Phantoms entered "and not you."

① 指信任

言谈举止（NO.952）

一个人说出的话儿，就话语本身——
也许——平静温和
却可能会给一颗蛰伏着的火星
提供了——导火索——

让我们的举止变得——老练——
让我们的言谈——谨慎周全——
炸药贮存于木炭——
在它点燃之前。

A Man may make a Remark —

In itself — a quiet thing

That may furnish the Fuse unto a Spark

In dormant nature — lain —

Let us deport — with skill —

Let us discourse — with care —

Powder exists in Charcoal —

Before it exists in Fire.

满足（NO.1036）

满足——意味着
餍饱——
欲求——是孜孜追求的无限的
代表。

占有，已是在我们达到目标
享受了销魂的时刻之后——
满足于永驻
并不可取。

Satisfaction — is the Agent
Of Satiety —
Want — a quiet Commissary
For Infinity.

To possess, is past the instant
We achieve the Joy —
Immortality contented
Were Anomaly.

生活是无限的（NO.1162）

我们现在所过的生活很是伟大。
我们将要看到的生活
更是超过现在，因为我们知道
生活是无限的。
可是当所有的空间都被览毕
所有的领域均已现露
人类所禀有的最小视野
也能把生活贬为无有。

The Life we have is very great.
The Life that we shall see
Surpasses it, we know, because
It is Infinity.
But when all Space has been beheld
And all Dominion shown
The smallest Human Heart's extent
Reduces it to none.

蜘蛛（NO.1167）

在一个我不愿讲出的环境
单枪匹马地
一只蜘蛛于我的缄默中
很卖劲地移挪

片刻的工夫它就在这里待得
比我还自如惬意
我觉得自己倒成了客人
于是匆匆地退了出来

为清点我的财产
我重访了故居
我发现它在悄然中好像成了
一个玩杂耍的处所
那里无需纳税也没有产权
悬于空气中的居住者们[①]
个个耀武扬威好像它们自己
都是特定的继承人——

① 指蜘蛛。

如果有人在街头动武

我可以还击——

如果有人侵占我的财产

以法律为依据

法规条律是我可求助的朋友

可是这又能如何匡正

对一个不属于这些范围内的侵犯

也即不在同一个水准——

这一由蜘蛛对心灵

对时日精髓之

侵占，噢主啊

我也许不该这样明指。

Alone and in a Circumstance
Reluctant to be told
A spider on my reticence
Assiduously crawled

And so much more at Home than I
Immediately grew
I felt myself a visitor
And hurriedly withdrew

Revisiting my late abode
With articles of claim
I found it quietly assumed
As a Gymnasium
Where Tax asleep and Title off
The inmates of the Air
Perpetual presumption took
As each were special Heir —

If any strike me on the street
I can return the Blow —
If any take my property
According to the Law
The Statute is my Learned friend
But what redress can be
For an offense nor here nor there
So not in Equity —
That Larceny of time and mind
The marrow of the Day
By spider, or forbid it Lord
That I should specify.

倘如我们没有那样去冒险（NO.1175）

我们对那种侥幸的脱险情有独钟
它仍能萦绕在脑际
在行为或事件过去很久以后
就像一阵阵的风吹来

倘如我们没有那样去冒险
风儿就不会有那般娇好
这轻风把它美妙的触须
从发根拂到我们的发梢

We like a Hairbreadth 'scape
It tingles in the Mind
Far after Act or Accident
Like paragraphs of Wind

If we had ventured less
The Breeze were not so fine
That reaches to our utmost Hair
Its Tentacles divine.

过去（NO.1203）

过去是这样一种奇怪的东西
对它的直面
可以给我们以销魂的时刻
或是羞愧感——

如果是毫无戒备的人碰到她[①]
我奉劝他还是快逃
她的虽已生锈的弹药
还是可能会开炮。

The Past is such a curious Creature
To look her in the Face
A Transport may receipt us
Or a Disgrace —

Unarmed if any meet her
I charge him fly
Her faded Ammunition
Might yet reply.

① 代指过去。

希冀（NO.1181）

在我希冀的时候我害怕——
希冀过后我敢于单人匹马
去到任何一个地块
犹如教堂尚在——
幽灵就不敢害人——
蛇莽就不能施淫——
体尝过厄运的人
就能抗过厄运——

When I hoped I feared —
Since I hoped I dared
Everywhere alone
As a Church remain —
Spectre cannot harm —
Serpent cannot charm —
He deposes Doom
Who hath suffered him —

沉默，缄默（NO.1251）

沉默是我们最为敬畏的。
在话语声中我们的心里觉得有着落——
然而缄默却是个无限
他自己没个脸儿。

Silence is all we dread.
There's Ransom in a Voice —
But Silence is Infinity.
Himself have not a face.

谜语（NO.1222）

对我们能猜出的谜语
我们很快就会不屑一顾——
昨日的惊喜离今天已经很远
已变得乏味和陈腐——

The Riddle we can guess
We speedily despise —
Not anything is stale so long
As Yesterday's surprise —

言语（NO.1212）

当言语已说出时
它已经死去，
有人说。

我说它才刚刚
开始了它的生命
自那一刻。

A word is dead
When it is said,
Some say.

I say it just
Begins to live
That day.

渴望（NO.1255）

渴望像是在泥土中
奋力挣扎的种子
相信只要它善于斡旋调停
最后总会顶出大地。

时辰，天气的阴晴雨雪——
对一切的情况都不了解，
这需要付出多少不懈的努力
在它见到天日之前！

Longing is like the Seed
That wrestles in the Ground,
Believing if it intercede
It shall at length be found.

The Hour, and the Clime —
Each Circumstance unknown,
What Constancy must be achieved
Before it see the Sun!

等待（NO.1277）

在我们对什么一直担着心的时候它来了——
不过它的到来倒使我们不再那么害怕
因为那么长时间的担心
几乎已经使得我们习惯了它——

不断的揣测——随后而致的沮丧——
揣测——而后的绝望——
等待什么东西的到来要比
知道它已在这儿更牵动心肠。

对事物极致的探试
刚刚到来的拂晓
比整个儿经历了它
更加的可怕难熬。

While we were fearing it, it came —
But came with less of fear
Because that fearing it so long
Had almost made it fair —

There is a Fitting — a Dismay —
A Fitting — a Despair
'Tis harder knowing it is Due
Than knowing it is Here.

They Trying on the Utmost
The Morning it is new
Is Terribler than wearing it
A whole existence through.

思想（NO.1452）

思想并非每天都有表达它的言词相随
它的来到，
像难解的信号——像啜饮
圣餐桌上的醇酒
在你品尝的时候你觉得它的味儿
来得那么醇，那么自然，
以致你不会想到它的珍贵，
和它的鲜至少见。

Your thoughts don't have words every day
They come a single time
Like signal esoteric sips
Of the communion Wine
Which while you taste so native seems
So easy so to be
You cannot comprehend its price
Nor its infrequency

当记忆扎根（NO.1508）

你不能使记忆生长
如果它的根儿已失——
拍实它四围的土壤
把它扶直
也许能欺骗了世人
可却救不回植物的生命——
真正的记忆，像雪松的足根
能穿透岩石无比坚硬——
你也不能将记忆砍掉
当它一旦已扎根生长——
任凭你刀砍斧劈
其钢芽铁花仍会开放——

You cannot make Remembrance grow
When it has lost its Root —
The tightening the Soil around
And setting it upright
Deceives perhaps the Universe
But not retrieves the Plant —
Real Memory, like Cedar Feet
Is shod with Adamant —
Nor can you cut Remembrance down
When it shall once have grown —
Its Iron Buds will sprout anew
However overthrown —

未知的世界（NO.1603）

从一个我们熟悉的世界去到
一个仍还未知的世界
就像一个孩子有时遇到的考验
他前面看到的是一座山脉，
山的后面是妖道横行
其他的情况一点不摸。
山那边的秘密是否能补偿了
他一个人对它的攀登呢？

The going from a world we know
To one a wonder still
Is like the child's adversity
Whose vista is a hill,
Behind the hill is sorcery
And everything unknown,
But will the secret compensate
For climbing it alone?

宛若青铜般——燃烧的火焰（NO.290）

宛若青铜般——燃烧的火焰——
在今夜的——北方——
它的展现——如此——恰当
如此镇定——和安详——
如此的高高在上，
全然漠视宇宙，和我——
它威严的光与影
感染了我单纯的心儿——
直到我的心胸豁然开朗——
在我的花梗上变得昂然向上——
蔑视世人和氧气的骄傲与狂妄——

我生命中的绚丽，是马戏巡回展——
它们无与伦比的表演
将愉悦若干个世纪
当我，早已成为萋萋荒草
之中的一座孤坟——
除了甲虫没有任何人——知晓。

Of Bronze — and Blaze —
The North — Tonight —
So adequate — it forms —
So preconcerted with itself —
So distant — to alarms —
An Unconcern so sovereign
To Universe, or me —
Infects my simple spirit
With Taints of Majesty —
Till I take vaster attitudes —
And strut upon my stem —
Disdaining Men, and Oxygen,
For Arrogance of them —

My Splendors, are Menagerie —
But their Competeless Show
Will entertain the Centuries
When I, am long ago,
An Island in dishonored Grass —
Whom none but Beetles — know.

我总感觉我失去了什么（NO.959）

我总感觉我失去了什么——
我被剥夺——是我最早的记忆
但被夺走了什么——我一无所知
那时我太年幼还不懂得猜疑

尽管如此，犹如徘徊在孩童中的
一个哀悼者，我走来走去
为失去的领地恸哭不已
是它流放了它唯一的王子——

如今老了，到了睿智的年龄
可也变得羸弱，因为智者多半如此——
但我发现我仍温馨地寻找着
我在放逐之前所拥有的殿宇——

而怀疑，像一根手指
时不时抚弄着我的额头
于是我朝着相反的方向
去把天国的位置寻找——

A loss of something ever felt I —
The first that I could recollect
Bereft I was — of what I knew not
Too young that any should suspect

A Mourner walked among the children
I notwithstanding went about
As one bemoaning a Dominion
Itself the only Prince cast out —

Elder, Today, a session wiser
And fainter, too, as Wiseness is —
I find myself still softly searching
For my Delinquent Palaces —

And a Suspicion, like a Finger
Touches my Forehead now and then
That I am looking oppositely
For the site of the Kingdom of Heaven —

像悲伤一样无迹可寻（NO.1540）

像悲伤一样无迹可寻
夏天离我们而去——
太难以觉察以至最后
不像是背信弃义——

寂静被蒸馏凸显了出来
当薄暮的微光早早就降临，
或是自然在独自消磨着
下午岑寂的光阴——

黄昏提前到来——
清晨显得陌生——
有礼，有种令人伤心的优雅，
犹如行将离去的，客人——

就这样，没有一片翅翼
没有一只舟楫
我们的夏季轻快地逃逸
消失在美的疆域。

As imperceptibly as Grief
The Summer lapsed away —
Too imperceptible at last
To seem like Perfidy —

A Quietness distilled
As Twilight long begun,
Or Nature spending with herself
Sequestered Afternoon —

The Dusk drew earlier in —
The Morning foreign shone —
A courteous, yet harrowing Grace,
As Guest, that would be gone —

And thus, without a Wing
Or service of a Keel
Our Summer made her light escape
Into the Beautiful.

风的职责很少（NO.1137）

风的职责很少，
把船掀翻，在海上，
创建三月，为洪水护航，
给自由导航。

风的乐趣很多，
他的居所无限的广阔，
或逗留，或游荡，
或沉思，或跟森林逗乐。

风的亲属是山巅
亚速海——昼夜平分点，
还有鸟儿与行星
和他互相致意、交谈。

风的局限
如果他真的有生，或有死，
他似乎太聪明罕有不清醒的时刻，
不过，我也只是猜测而已。

The duties of the Wind are few,
To cast the ships, at Sea,
Establish March, the Floods escort,
And usher Liberty.

The pleasures of the Wind are broad,
To dwell Extent among,
Remain, or wander,
Speculate, or Forests entertain.

The kinsmen of the Wind are Peaks
Azof — the Equinox,
Also with Bird and Asteroid
A bowing intercourse.

The limitations of the Wind
Do he exist, or die,
Too wise he seems for Wakelessness,
However, know not I.

图书在版编目（CIP）数据

这世界，静默如初：狄金森经典诗选：全2册 /（美）狄金森著；王晋华译 .—北京：台海出版社，2017.7

ISBN 978-7-5168-1459-8

Ⅰ.①这… Ⅱ.①狄… ②王… Ⅲ.①诗集－美国－近代 Ⅳ.①I712.24

中国版本图书馆 CIP 数据核字（2017）第 149013 号

这世界，静默如初：狄金森经典诗选（上）

著　　者：［美］狄金森　　译　　者：王晋华

监　　制：薛　婷　　策划编辑：褚宇恒　　责任编辑：俞滟荣

版式设计：北京大观世纪文化传媒有限公司　　责任印制：蔡　旭

出版发行：台海出版社

地　　址：北京市东城区景山东街 20 号　　邮政编码：100009

电　　话：010-64041652（发行，邮购）

传　　真：010-84045799（总编室）

网　　址：www. taimeng.org.cn/thcbs/default.htm

E－mail：thcbs@126.com

经　　销：全国各地新华书店

印　　刷：北京瑞禾彩色印刷有限公司

本书如有破损、缺页、装订错误，请与本社联系调换

开　　本：880mm×1230mm　　1/32

字　　数：340 千字　　印　张：18.5

版　　次：2018 年 3 月第 1 版　　印　次：2018 年 3 月第 1 次印刷

书　　号：ISBN 978-7-5168-1459-8

定　　价：84. 00 元（全 2 册）